# Tempt Me Please, Cowboy

# Tempt Me Please, Cowboy

## An 85th Copper Mountain Rodeo Romance

Megan Crane

TULE
PUBLISHING

Tempt Me Please, Cowboy


Tule Publishing First Printing, September 2023

The Tule Publishing, Inc.



First Publication by Tule Publishing 2023

Cover design by Lee Hyat Designs



ISBN: 978-1-961544-52-9

# Acknowledgement

*To Jane, again, for everything.*

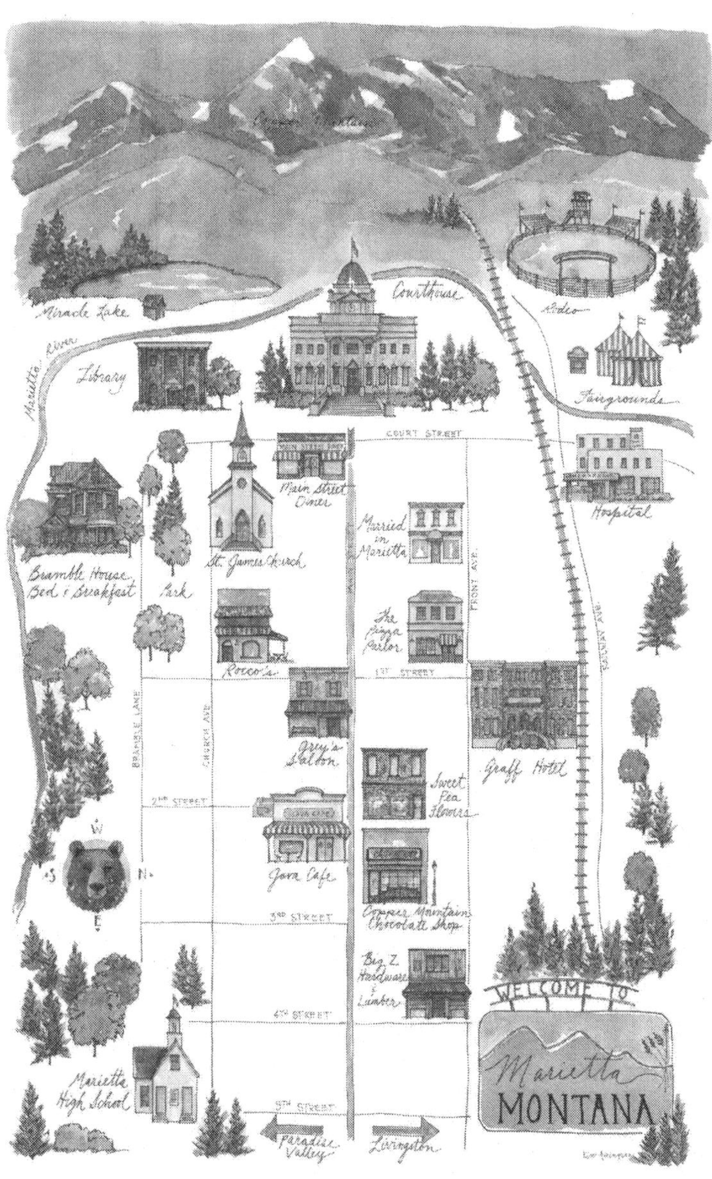
Courthouse
Miracle Lake
Rodeo
Marietta River
Library
Fairgrounds
COURT STREET
Main Street Diner
Hospital
Married in Marietta
Bramble House Bed & Breakfast
Park
St. James Church
The Pizza Parlor
FRONT AVE.
Rocco's
1ST STREET
BRAMBLE LANE
CHURCH AVE.
Grey's Saloon
Graff Hotel
Sweet Pea Flowers
2ND STREET
W
S
N
E
Java Cafe
3RD STREET
Copper Mountain Chocolate Shop
Big Z Hardware & Lumber
WELCOME TO
4TH STREET
Marietta
MONTANA
Marietta High School
5TH STREET
Paradise Valley
Livingston

# Chapter One

HE WAS EXACTLY the kind of trouble she needed.

Six feet and then some of lean muscle packed into jeans, boots, and a white T-shirt that every woman in a ten-mile radius of Grey's Saloon here in Marietta, Montana, was going to dream about tonight.

Herself included.

And that wasn't even getting to the dirty-blond hair, a little too long and the kind of messy that led straight to more dreaming, plus a set of amused green eyes that were a health hazard all their own.

Sydney Campbell stopped pretending to do her brand-new job as the worst bartender in the history of the old saloon that had been in her family since a branch of Greys escaped the east. They'd found Paradise Valley and decided that looking for copper in the nearby hills was thirsty work. Better still, that they should address that problem. They'd been doing exactly that ever since.

She paid no attention to her uncle Jason's irritated muttering about firing her even though he'd only just grudgingly hired her in the first place. Because unlike the many people packed into this place tonight who were very careful with the current proprietor and his legendary bad mood of about twenty years and counting, *she* knew he was all bark.

Well. Mostly.

And anyway, she wasn't the only person staring.

Because she wasn't the only person in the saloon with eyes.

"I'm supposed to be doing normal things like normal people," she reminded her uncle when he scowled at her, and then smiled angelically at him when that scowl deepened.

"I didn't realize 'normal' was on the table," he growled.

But he left her to it.

This was the main benefit of letting her entire, over-involved extended family think that she was having a nervous breakdown. That her arrival in town heralded an epic collapse of uncertain nature. That she was *in the throes* of a cataclysmic personal event.

Sydney hadn't meant to let them all think that. Not really. But she hadn't corrected them, either.

What else could explain her sudden decision to relocate to tiny little Marietta for an indeterminate amount of time this fall? Sydney usually only came to Montana for Christmas, family weddings, peremptory summons from her perpetually unamused grandmother, and the like. She flew in, smiled like a well-adjusted and potentially well-rounded person for no more than a long weekend, and then flew back to reality on the red-eye.

Because the reality for most of her adult life was that she

was busy, and not in the way everyone liked to claim they were *so busy so busy so busy* these days. Sydney spent night and day in her office at Langley, where she rarely knew or cared if it was night or day because she was lost in all the data that was always scrolling across her many screens and through her head. She was the kind of busy that when her phone buzzed, she always had to answer it, and she was expected to appear in a nearby office within minutes or at the Pentagon within the hour.

She was so busy that when she actually got to go home, she sometimes had to take a minute or five to remember that yes, in fact, she had a small, soulless apartment in nearby McLean, VA, chosen years back so that she was never *too* far from work. But she was usually *at* work, so every time she actually went back "home" she felt as if she was staying in a hotel. She'd never bothered to put up pictures or decorate. It had come finished and she left it that way because it was easier. No muss, no fuss.

She had no pets. She saw no people outside of work because she had no time to see anyone. Her friends and family had to content themselves with erratic phone calls and texts at odd hours.

Only other people with all-consuming jobs understood what it was like, and that it wasn't sad. That she was not depressed or riddled with ulcers or whatever they liked to think, simply because her job was the significant and consuming relationship in her life and had been since she'd been recruited out of Georgetown. Everyone else used words like "workaholic" and "stress case" and so on, never understanding that those were compliments in Sydney's world.

Some of her friends and family claimed she was a spy. Others preferred to call her a flake.

Sydney was neither, but she neither confirmed nor denied it when people said these things to her face. She could only imagine what they said when she wasn't around, because she knew her family enjoyed nothing more than diving deep into the psychoanalysis. Preferably over drinks served right here in this saloon.

It wasn't a stretch for them to imagine it had all become too much for her, because they thought it *should have* been too much for her years ago.

That wasn't the truth of things, not precisely, but Sydney had decided to go with it and it had already borne some pretty excellent fruit. Her cousins, usually notable for their benign mockery and sarcastic references to everything under the sun and especially to each other, were forced instead to attempt pleasantries. They'd gotten the news through the lightning-fast Grey family grapevine last night and had called her in a wave earlier today.

Most of them were bad at pleasantries, being genetically predetermined toward intensity.

Or maybe they were just unused to Sydney actually answering her phone.

What she'd realized was that she should have pretended

to be fragile years ago. It was hilarious.

But tonight, she wasn't feeling the least bit fragile.

She tracked his progress through the saloon. Slow and lazy and intent all at once, just like him.

When she'd met him the first time, long ago, she had not been pretending to be fragile. She barely knew that word. That night she'd been after oblivion and she'd managed to get a fairly good grip on it. It was the night before Christmas that year, and she'd squeaked into town last minute on a flight that had skated into Bozeman—and bounced a few times while it was at it—right before they'd started cancelling all flights coming in and out ahead of an expected snowstorm in the mountains.

Sydney had decided that instead of attempting the drive out to Big Sky, where her grandparents lived and hosted Christmas almost every year, she would stay in Marietta and head over very early in the morning with her uncle after he handled the booming Christmas Eve business at Grey's Saloon. When they could see how bad the storm was going to be, since there was a big gap between *newscaster bad* and *real Montanan bad.*

Besides, she had discovered over time that everyone benefited when she put some space between her job and her family, since her family liked to talk about her career like it was her toxic boyfriend.

Some people called it "blowing off steam" and that night, Sydney had gotten into the tequila to see just how steamy she could get. And she'd been having a grand old time. She'd been hanging out with a girl she'd used to play with in summers long past, when her airy, careless mother would park her kids in Montana for most of June, July, and August and take off to follow her bliss—meaning her latest lover—wherever it took her.

Sydney and Emmy Mathis had been summer friends. Close when they saw each other and fine when they didn't, and Sydney had been delighted to discover that held true once they were grown, too. Emmy now lived in town because she'd married the one and only Griffin Hyatt, another summer-in-Marietta guy who was now a tattoo artist at such a high level that people traveled from all over the world to little Marietta, Montana, for a little ink directly from his hand. He and Emmy had come out with a circle of friends as well as their sharp-eyed grandmothers—who drank more than everyone else—and they'd all been in a festive mood that Christmas Eve.

The Grans, as the grandmothers were known all over Crawford County, had been drinking all of Griffin's tattooed and bearded friends under the table. Emmy had long since shifted to Cokes. Sydney couldn't really say how many shots she'd had, which to her mind was the point and purpose of shots. That was the sort of data she didn't need to hold on to, so she didn't. It was all part and parcel of the Christmas spirit.

Though she did remember, with perfect clarity, when

she'd decided she needed to step outside to see if a burst of frigid air might sober her up a little before her uncle Jason cut her off. Something she had no doubt he would then want to discuss before dawn as they inched through new-fallen snow all the way to Big Sky, no thank you.

That was what she told herself, but it wasn't really the reason. He would cut her off when he felt like it no matter what state she was in, and his lectures did not require an inciting incident. The real reason was that Sydney wasn't a sentimental person. She wasn't forever surfing about on the tides of various emotions like Melody, her impossibly dramatic mother, who Sydney loved dearly and also was very happy to see but rarely.

*She* wasn't like her mother. She could never be so careless and emotional. *She* didn't like to think about the fact that the air was just… different in Marietta. That even in the crystal clear cold of that December night with a storm sitting heavy in the hills, there was something about standing outside and taking such a deep breath that it was like inhaling the stars.

Sydney didn't wax poetic. She dealt in facts. She put data and details together, synthesized seemingly unrelated tidbits of information, and drew connections no one else saw.

That was some damn fine poetry right there.

But she didn't let herself think things like that and she certainly didn't say things like that, so she'd told the alarmingly clear-eyed Grans that she was getting some air.

*Of course you are, dear,* Gran Martha Hyatt had said serenely. *That will freeze the alcohol right out of your bloodstream, I'm sure.*

*Perhaps it's not the alcohol that needs the breathing room,* Gran Harriet Mathis had added in a similar tone.

Both with smiles that Sydney had chosen to ignore, because the old women were knowing and strange but they didn't *actually know* anything about her. No one did, and not because she was secretive, as her older sister Devyn liked to claim. But because there was nothing to know about her except what was classified, and anyone who needed to know that already did.

She had hurtled for the door to the outside, maybe a little too desperate to get away from those knowing old lady smiles, thrown it open to charge straight out, and had instead slammed into the person coming in.

Directly into him.

So hard that he'd had to take a step back and grip her by the arms to keep them both from toppling over and doing a header on the icy sidewalk, straight into the snow.

But he had risen to the occasion, instantly.

She thought about that now as he did his usual thing, wandering through the saloon, greeting people he knew, and pretending he didn't know exactly where Sydney was. Or notice that she was looking right at him.

Sometimes she was the one who pretended not to see him, and that was fun too.

But either way, she knew this game. And every time they played it, everything in her turned bright and achingly hot with that same longing that had rushed into her on a cold sidewalk in December, filling her up in place of all those Christmas stars, an intoxicant all its own.

That first night, they had stayed out in the dark together, holding on to each other a whole lot longer than necessary to simply remain upright. Sydney had been laughing, telling herself it was all that tequila, and he'd looked a little bit like he'd been punched straight in the face.

Like he was dazed, somehow, and not from their collision.

He wasn't fragile either.

And it was true that she'd spent a lot of time in the years since, five years to be exact, thinking about that particular poleaxed expression he'd wore in those first frigid moments. She remembered them as a blinding rush of heat. She didn't have a lot of nights in that bed of hers in her barely used apartment. She mostly slept, when and if she slept, on the couch in her office or on the floor. And yet every single one of the nights she actually went home involved her lying in that strange bed, pretending to sleep, running through moments like that one.

Almost like she was analyzing them. Looking for connections. Drawing conclusions.

*You're going to catch a chill and freeze to death,* he'd said, *and it will be my fault for letting you stand out here without a coat.*

She'd learned so many things about him in that moment. It was his voice. She heard the Texas in it. The drawl. She already knew that he was strong because she could feel it all around her. He could have lifted her straight up from the ground if he'd wanted and she had the happy little notion that he did want that. She knew that he was taller than her. She knew he was chiseled to perfection, there in jeans and boots that told truths about his form and the heavy coat he'd already unzipped, happily, so she could see there were no lies on the rest of him.

He was all muscle. All man.

There was no getting past the fact that he was wildly, astonishingly hot. She'd told herself then and later that it was the tequila and maybe that had helped, but it had been five years now. There was no getting around the fact that it was him, too.

And that little hint of Texas was like hot sauce on top, making everything smoke.

*I'm from generations of good Montana stock,* she had replied, smiling wildly for no good reason. *I'm not saying I'm going to take a nap in a snowbank, but I'm also not going to freeze to death in three seconds.*

*I'm from Texas, darlin',* he'd said, in case she hadn't worked that out. *And I might.*

He hadn't let go and she hadn't pushed the issue, because she really didn't want him to let go. She liked that he'd called her *darlin'* like that, like she was the kind of woman men used endearments on when she knew she wasn't. She never had been. Sydney was spiky, combative, blunt. Everyone told her so at work, and those were compliments.

But he'd drawled out *darlin'* like he meant it. And she'd watched, outside in the hushed dark of Marietta on a Christmas Eve with a storm coming in, the way the corner of his mouth had curled.

Just a little bit.

As if it was hers alone.

Looking back, she liked to think it was the tequila talking when she'd grinned up at him, opened up her mouth, and said, *But if you're worried, we could always warm each other up.*

Like she was the kind of *darlin'* who flirted with men that way.

Or at all.

But that night, she had been. And her reward was that she'd watched his dark green gaze go smoky like his voice.

*Glad I was here to keep you out of that snowbank,* he'd drawled. *I'm Jackson Flint.*

And he'd been warming her up ever since.

Jackson had been a newcomer in Marietta back then, the previously unknown half-brother to the Flint brothers—who were famous billionaires out of Texas, according to all the gossip Sydney had ever heard about them. Jonah Flint still did his Texas thing, though he also spent a lot of his time over near Flathead Lake, where he had a whole lot of land

and the sort of ranch men like him used for extended business retreats. Because men like him had time for extended business trips, their currency being money and power. Not information and the element of surprise, the currency Sydney knew best.

It was Jonah's twin Jasper Flint that folks in Marietta knew best, because he'd come in and bought the old train depot out from under the nose of the many history buffs in sprawling Crawford County. He'd also helped—Sydney's family muttered that really, he'd entirely funded—the turning of the old Crawford mansion up on a hill above town into a museum that commemorated the sometimes shady doings of old Black Bart. Black Bart had been the Crawford ancestor who settled in the town right about the time the Greys started slinging drinks, but he'd gone more railroad baron than barkeep.

Jasper had opened up FlintWorks Brewery after he'd walked away from Texas, brewing his own beer and ale and winning awards for his trouble. He'd made the place family friendly, with food and music until early evening, when families could head home and anyone looking for trouble could head for the other bars in town that catered to it. Jasper had then gone on to win the town's heart because he'd married Chelsea Crawford Collier herself, who had been a schoolteacher when he'd met her—if struggling with the weight of her late mama's expectations regarding the Crawford legacy, according to all sources—and was now the mayor.

*Guess she sorted out that legacy,* Sydney had said when her aunt Gracie had filled her in on this tidbit.

*She lives up in the old mansion now, the part that isn't a museum, and was elected in a landslide,* her uncle Ryan had said with a laugh. *It feels like a full Marietta circle.*

Not that Jackson had known any of that back then on that frigid Christmas Eve. After years of acquiescing to his mother's feelings about their shared father, not a good man at all, he'd come to Montana to see if his brothers were worth getting to know.

*They're all right,* Jackson had told Sydney, gruffly, when she'd seen him again after that first Christmas.

They hadn't kept in touch after that wild, explosive night together. They hadn't even exchanged numbers. It felt like pure chance that Sydney had ended up coming back to Montana that year for one of her cousins' weddings that so many of them liked to hold here in Marietta for a variety of sentimental reasons that Sydney only pretended to understand.

But she'd walked into Grey's and there he'd been. And it was only once he'd smiled at her in that slow, hot, bone-melting way of his that she'd accepted that the prospect of seeing him again was the entire reason she'd decided to go into Grey's in the first place that night.

*I'm glad to know that they're not too bad,* she'd said. *For billionaires.*

She'd let him buy her a drink. She'd let their fingers

brush, so the heat of it could gallop through her. And she'd very much enjoyed letting her imagination run wild with all the things he could do next.

And then he did them.

All of them.

The same way he did every time she'd made it back to Montana since. He had turned into a staple of her trips out west. See a little family, enjoy Jackson and all his many talents, and look forward to the next time without ever knowing when that was going to come.

But this time she wasn't here for a couple of days here, a long holiday weekend there.

This time, she was staying for the season.

*What you mean you're staying in the Graff?* her grandmother had demanded when Sydney had called to tell her she was coming to town and staying a while. *You can't stay in a* hotel. *You are a* Grey, *Sydney. What will people think?*

*I don't know any of the people you mean,* Sydney had replied blandly. *So I couldn't speculate as to their thoughts, Grandma.*

Elly Grey, never a cozy grandmother at the best of times, had not appreciated that remark.

But Sydney had no intention of giving up a hotel room in the gorgeous old Graff, renovated by local hero Troy Sheenan a decade back to make the most of its Old West splendor, especially when there was the very real possibility of ghosts. Besides, the rooms in the old hotel were pretty and bursting with character, unlike her sad apartment back east.

And anyway, the family options available to her were not appealing. She could stay out in Big Sky with her prickly grandparents, no thank you. She could bunk down in one of Uncle Jason's back rooms at the bar or one of her cousins' old rooms in his house of bitterness, another hard pass. She could immerse herself in the chaos of her cousin Luce's life now that she was divorced and forever at war with her ex, complete with her teenage sons stampeding about, but that sounded possibly the worst of all.

Her cousin Christina was over in the Bitterroot Valley and she'd wondered if she should head that way for a little change of pace, but Christina and her husband Dare were neck deep in the small kid thing and Sydney knew herself far too well to imagine that she could suddenly bloom into a nanny sort of person. Even indirectly. Her aunt Gracie and Uncle Ryan had offered their guest room, but Sydney had told them she didn't want to put them out by being there on the rare occasions they weren't off leading their outdoor and adventure trips that ran all year.

This was all perfectly true. But she understood, now that she had Jackson in her sights again, that her decision had really had very little to do with putting out her family members.

It was that she didn't want to have a discussion with any of them about where she might be at night. Or who she was with.

Because she fully expected it would be with him.

Jackson Flint, who was, she could admit it, the main reason she hadn't thought too hard about it when her boss had suggested she take a few months off to run through the vacation days she'd been accruing for years. And to get her head on straight, in his words.

Sydney knew perfectly well her head didn't need straightening. Her head was on just fine. Her boss knew it too, but had to suggest otherwise. And because they dealt in innuendo and making connections between possibilities, there was no need to spell things out.

Sometimes things happened that everybody needed space from. And sometimes, when her work embarrassed the wrong people, it was the kind of space that necessitated that she not show her face where said people might see it.

She might have been a little more worked up about the injustice of that, but the minute her boss had started talking about *taking the season*—coincidentally, the exact amount of time it would take before the particular official who didn't want his failures looking back at him with Sydney's face to move on to his next post—she'd started thinking of a whole fall in Montana.

And not just Marietta, this place her family had helped found and where Greys had lived ever since, as ubiquitous as Copper Mountain that stood sentry over the town and the stretch of mountains that cluttered up the horizons. She loved her family as much as she was capable of loving anything, but really, it had been Jackson who flashed in her mind.

He was why she'd figured she could handle a season away from the job.

She'd spent her first night out in Big Sky explaining to her grandmother why she wasn't staying there until New Year's, which had gone even worse in person. Today she'd fielded phone calls from her sister and all the Grey cousins while checking herself into the Graff and then convincing Uncle Jason to give her a job.

Because she needed *something* to do. She wasn't a *sit around and relax* kind of person.

And then she'd waited.

Because she and Jackson never called each other, though they had broken the no-phone-numbers barrier some years back. What usually happened was that they saw each other, then they set each other on fire.

Again and again and again, until she had to go.

It was the perfect system, in Sydney's mind.

So she settled in and watched as Jackson did his thing. He was like a slow-moving comet streaking his way through the crowd of people, that much brighter and that much hotter than everything and anything around him. She could hardly keep her eyes off him, but then again, she wasn't trying that hard.

She found herself smiling as he took his sweet time making his way over to the bar.

But when he did, it was like everything else fell away except the two of them.

"They'll hire anyone around here," Jackson drawled, his green gaze already hot and deliciously dark.

"It's a shocking example of nepotism," Sydney replied, nodding her head in agreement. "I'm personally appalled."

She pulled him out a bottle of beer, not the kind his family brewed over at FlintWorks, where he'd been running things for a few years now. She even opened it before she slid it across the bar to him.

"Mighty obliged, darlin'." He was all drawl.

"I live to serve, cowboy."

His eyes gleamed. "Do you now."

And for moment they stood there, in the heat of it.

Jackson took a swig of his beer and set it back down on the polished wood surface. Sydney leaned forward, sure that he was about to offer one of his invitations. They were always hot. And he always delivered.

She found herself forced to admit that if he hadn't come in tonight, she would have had to break protocol entirely and go looking for him.

Looking at him now, she wasn't sure why she hadn't started that way.

There weren't a whole lot of things she wouldn't do to hear this man call her *darlin'* in that way he did.

She was already thinking of all things she could do in return. All the things she *would* do. Her hands on his body.

Her mouth moving like fire over his skin.

Every time she saw him, she couldn't believe that she'd made it so long between hits.

Sydney remembered where she was, barely, and made sure that her uncle was down at the other end of the bar, out of earshot.

"I have a room at the Graff," she said.

She watched Jackson take that information on board. Because by now, he knew things about her. Like that she always stayed with family when she was in town.

He took his time tasting his beer. "You always say that your apartment in DC feels like a hotel room." And that was disconcerting. She didn't remember telling him that. Then again, she supposed there was more talking on the nights she'd spent with him than she cared to remember. Because there were so many more interesting things to focus on. "You trying to see if there's some difference between the two?"

"The Graff is a much nicer hotel. My apartment can only dream of such splendor."

He looked at her, his green eyes steady, bright, expectant. Almost as if he thought she was going to *say something.*

And suddenly, for no reason she cared to examine, Sydney felt nervous. That was the only possible explanation for the sudden dizzy feeling in her belly, like a swarm of butterflies.

The analytical part of her, that in every other place but this one was the only part of her, kicked in. Hard. What did she actually know about Jackson Flint? Her personal policy was not to dig into people she knew in real life, because that was creepy, and she'd held to that. For all she knew he had a wife. Four kids. Whole other lives.

Something deep in her gut told her that was impossible, but wasn't that exactly what the other woman in all those scenarios *wanted* to think?

Then again, Sydney didn't actually need to run a background check on Jackson Flint. That's what a close-knit town like Marietta was for. If he was a bad one, someone would have mentioned it in Sydney's hearing. She'd never asked and no one had ever confronted her, but she was fairly certain more than one member of her family had seen her talking to him in the saloon before.

Still, she was forced to acknowledge the unfortunate reality that she had no idea how Jackson was going to take the news she was about to impart.

Maybe he liked her only enough for a couple of nights a year. Maybe he didn't want any more than that. He'd never indicated that he did. She'd always found that evidence of his superiority over all other men. She'd loved that it was part and parcel of their hands-off approach, because it made their hands-on times that much more exciting.

But this was different. She hadn't really let herself think about what his reaction to that difference might be.

Or how she would respond to it if it was… not great.

"I'm going to stay a while," she made herself say, because

she was blunt and abrasive and prickly, and she thought those were positive things. She said things that other people didn't say. She was paid for that. She was good at that.

She was so good at that she'd been sent on paid leave.

Suddenly it seemed, in that moment, *critically important* that she remember the things that she was good at.

Jackson had no reaction to what she said, which seemed like a reaction all its own. He stared back at her for so long that she began to wonder if she hadn't spoken at all. If she'd only intended to and the words were still sitting there on her tongue.

He looked away for a moment, then down at his beer. He fiddled with it as if he was going to pick it up and take another pull, but he didn't.

"Define 'a while,'" he suggested.

"You know," she said in a breezy sort of way that wasn't her at all. "A season."

"An actual season? Meaning three months? The fall equinox right on to the winter solstice? That season? Because it hasn't actually started yet. It's still technically summer."

"That's maybe overly precise." She thought about how she'd been sitting in her boss's office, the sun she rarely felt on her actual skin beaming in, thinking of Jackson. But she had been thinking of him naked. She had been thinking of him *after* this conversation. She had not thought about having to live through this conversation at all. "Until New Year's, I expect."

"New Year's," he repeated. "It's going to be Labor Day on Monday, Sydney."

"I had no idea you were so interested in the calendar." And maybe that was a little too much edge in her voice, but this was the strangest conversation she'd ever had with him. And did not appear to have anything to do with climbing him like a tree, her favorite and really only leisure activity. "Or equinoxes, solstices, and public holidays, for that matter."

"I'm interested in all kinds of things."

Jackson's voice went lower, and that was better, but also worse. There was a different heat, then.

He was studying her in a way that made her feel prickly all over, and only partially because she didn't like being the subject of that kind of investigation. She was the one who collected data points. She didn't care for the notion that he was the one doing the collecting. Or that she was providing any usable data to him in the first place.

"So if I'm following this, you woke up one morning and thought what the hell, then threw in your fancy DC life of secrets to be a barmaid?"

"A bartender, thank you. Even *barkeep* would do, for that archaic flair. I think you know as well as I do that my uncle Jason isn't about to let anyone treat me or anyone else behind this bar like a *barmaid*."

"But that's what you're going to do for *the season*. You will live in a tiny town in Montana, serve folks drinks, and wait for the new year."

"Some people would call that a life of ease and relaxation."

"Would you?"

She wanted him to call her *darlin'* again. It was beginning to feel actively oppressive that instead he was… *quizzing* her on something she had no intention of talking about. Sydney hadn't realized that it would require this much *talking* anyway.

"My family is under the impression that I'm having a nervous breakdown." She smirked a little, hoping that was a little softer than all the edges poking around inside her now. "I may have given them that impression."

"Are you?"

Direct and to the point. That was the thing about Jackson that drew her in, time and again. There was the drawl and all that magic he could conjure with his hands, his mouth. But when it mattered, he didn't beat around the bush.

"I don't believe so," she said, because she could admire the directness even while wondering why they were standing here having a casual conversation when they could be talking about when and how they could tear each other's clothes off. Or better yet, doing it. "I'm thinking of developing a drinking problem, though. It's expected. It would seem odd if I didn't, don't you think?"

Once again, it was like he was seeing inside her skin. As

if there were hieroglyphics there that only he could read, and she should have found that alarming. Instead, it made her glow, inside and out, with a particular wild heat that settled heavy between her legs.

His smile was made of fire and glory, and it was the best thing she'd seen in months. She felt it go through her like a new heat all its own.

"Darlin'," he said—at last—and she felt that shiver all over her like the first caress of the night, "I have a much better idea. Get drunk on me."

And for the first time since she'd got on that plane at Washington Dulles, aware that she was facing down an unprecedented four months of workless freedom—a nightmare by any reckoning—Sydney thought to herself that this Montana might just work out after all.

# Chapter Two

JACKSON FLINT HAD been born a long shot, so that made him well and truly prepared to play the long game. Here and everywhere.

Sydney might not know it—he figured she didn't want to know—but he'd been playing this game with her for some while. And four months instead of the usual four days looked to Jackson like an opportunity, and he hadn't gotten where he was today by ignoring opportunity when it came knocking.

He didn't intend to start now.

Her uncle got a little growly—or more than usual—until Sydney actually set about tending bar, but that was a good thing. It gave Jackson another opportunity, this time to really think about what she'd told him.

*I'm going to stay a while.*

He was used to four days at most. Four days if he was lucky and she was never that happy about it. She started to get twitchy within hours and by day three, she was already responding to work messages no matter who she promised she wouldn't.

Jackson had decided a long while back that it was better

to be the guy who relaxed her and made her smile. Not one of the many people who made her so twitchy that she'd been known to change her flights to go home early.

If he'd learned one thing from his mama it was that love wasn't something that you could grip on to unless it gripped you right back. He'd kept his palms open, hoping she would find her way back to him, and she always did.

But four months was the kind of time a man could really sink his fingers into. It was the kind of time that could change everything.

Jackson intended to do exactly that.

Every time he saw her, he waited to see if she affected him a little less. He waited to see if looking at her didn't set up that racket inside him, that deep kind of humming that made every bit of bone and flesh he had take notice.

But it was always the same.

Usually, it was worse.

The thing about Sydney Campbell was that she'd been a wrecking ball from the first glance.

All these years later he was not only picking up the pieces, he was still trying to figure out what in the hell he was supposed to do about it.

Tonight seemed as decent a time to figure it out as any.

Jackson took his beer and moved away from the bar, biting back a grin at the panicked look Sydney sent after him as she tried to take a new rush of orders. The usual Friday night crowd was kicking up their heels with a whole lot more tourists and visitors woven in the way they were all summer, but especially in the run up to the rodeo. This year the mayor had told them all to expect more rodeo traffic than usual, since it was Copper Mountain Rodeo's landmark 85$^{th}$ year.

He liked that people here cared about that. In fact, Jackson found he liked Montana a whole lot more than he'd expected he would, what with all that Texas dirt in his veins. No one had been more surprised than him that he'd made it through his first winter, ready for more. And it wasn't like he'd taken the easy way through that winter the way he could have. His brother Jonah had offered the use of a whole guest cottage on his land out by Flathead Lake, but Jackson had declined.

There was good, hard ranch work all over the place in these parts, and he'd introduced himself to Marietta that way, riding out his first long, cold winter as a ranch hand. At the same time that he and his brother Jasper, and only sometimes the far more forbidding Jonah, were taking each other's measure, Jackson was out there showing folks who he was with his hands and his strong back, his dependability and his willingness to stay until the job was finished, no matter what.

All the things that had always served him well in all the various lives he'd lived along the way.

What that had also meant was that he'd gotten to know the fine people of Crawford County and a host of others spread out through Paradise Valley in a way he never could have if he'd stayed in town.

So there were any numbers of backs to slap, shoulders to bump, and easy conversations for him to slide into with only part of his attention while he mulled over the Sydney problem in his head.

Because looking back, he wasn't sure just when it had dawned on him that Sydney had put a substantial dent in his romantic life.

He wasn't the biggest sinner around, though he was certainly no saint, but he'd been focused on the complications of having thin Texas blood in the harsh Montana winter when he'd first met her. And there'd been hard work to do, both out on the ranches that had hired his labor and with his half brothers. Who hadn't treated him badly, necessarily, but also hadn't taken too kindly to the news that the father they didn't think highly of had been even worse than they'd thought.

There had been a lot to think about, that was all, and it had seemed like no time at all for the thaw to come in. The mountains began to let go of some of their snowcaps. And then Sydney was back again one night, gazing at him from behind those bangs he thought about way too much. With those clever eyes of hers and that wicked smile to match. She still wasn't his type. He'd thought that from the first. She was skinny and edgy when he'd always gravitated to rounder and softer. She had that red hair and those dark eyes when he liked them Texas tacky with the big blonde hair, the blue eyes to match, and a good old pageant queen smile.

But the thing about Sydney was, one look at her and no one else would do.

Even tonight, while she was under the same roof for a change, he was aware of how messed up this whole thing was. The saloon was filled with friends and acquaintances, and he thought pretty much all of them had tried to set him up with a sister, a buddy, or a good friend of their wives' at one point or another.

It had taken him years to admit to himself why it was he had always declined.

And longer still to face himself in the mirror and ask what, exactly, he planned to do about the situation.

But there hadn't been an answer. Because what he knew about her life in Washington DC, was that it was brutal and constant and she rarely pulled herself away from it. The family members who tried to make her always ended up frustrated, and Sydney never seemed to care.

*They all love me,* she'd told him once, wrapped up in his arms in the big bed that took up too much of the floor space in his big studio apartment above the old train depot building. *They just think I love my job more than I love them.*

*Do you?* he'd asked. What he'd meant was, *do you love your job more than me?*

But he was a grown man who knew better than to say things like that out loud.

Hell, he wasn't sure he liked knowing something like that was floating around inside him like a cartoon bomb with a loud ticking noise and a flashing countdown. What if it went off?

*They have spouses, families, all that stuff,* she'd replied, her eyes sultry as she leaned in to press her lips into the place where his neck and his shoulder blade met. *I have work. They're allowed to like their stuff. I'm not allowed to like mine. Isn't that weird?*

And he didn't want to be another thing this woman could *seem not to care about*, so he'd grunted some or other assent and then rolled her over, because she cared about the things they did together. She cared about the fires he lit and the way the two of them burned so bright together. He knew that much.

Sometimes he figured it was more than most people got, so it ought to be enough.

And if it never felt like enough, well. That was something he'd had a long time to learn how to keep to himself.

Jackson settled in at a noisy table filled with some of the men he'd worked with out on the area ranches, and let their exuberant discussion of the upcoming Copper Mountain Rodeo—and which locals they reckoned might bring the town a little glory—cover the fact that he was doing a little brooding of his own.

At least this time, sitting here with Sydney on his mind, she was here too.

He had to consider that an upgrade.

He studied her as she moved around behind the bar, laughing at her own mistakes while her uncle glowered, and looked as if he would've preferred straight up torture to his niece's invasion of his space. Though it was plain to Jackson that none of the men she was serving felt the same.

Then again, he already had it bad.

Because watching her concentrate, fiercely, was a whole body experience. He could almost *see* the gears turning in that remarkable mind of hers. She frowned, focusing intently she tried to mimic something Jason was doing beside her.

The last time Jackson his seen her focusing like that she'd been naked with her legs draped over his shoulders, her hands up above her head to grip the headboard, watching him as he slid himself deep inside her, then out again.

He had to look away and spend a few moments thinking about things like the process of gelding before he embarrassed himself.

She liked to treat him like they were strangers, even though, every time she came into town, she was in his arms within hours. It had taken him years to get her number, though he didn't use it. Just a text every now and again, usually on her birthday. Something to remind her that he was still here.

Not waiting. Not exactly.

Though he could admit that he'd started wondering if he'd ever get an opportunity like this.

"I hear Rye Calhoun is going to ride a few bulls next week," Trey Sheenan said then, drawing Jackson's attention back to the table. Though he didn't recognize the name.

"He hasn't thrown his hat in the ring in a long time," ex-rodeo champ Sam Wyatt replied.

"Have to be pretty brave to step up to the Copper Mountain ring with so many rodeo stars scattered all over Paradise Valley," Jackson drawled.

Sam's brother Joe eyed him. "Feeling brave, Flint?"

"Feeling glad I have a bar to run," Jackson replied, with a grin that made them all laugh.

But internally, he was doing what he always did. He was stacking up all the things he knew about Sydney Campbell and laying them out like he might need to play them like cards later. He'd always been good at cards. Particularly poker.

She was one of the Grey cousins who swept in and out of town like the weather, usually in packs, and often in the company of Luce, the only one in their generation who'd settled down in town. It was surprising that Luce herself wasn't around tonight, but then, that oldest son of hers was nineteen these days, and a problem. Knowing the only local Grey cousin, she was off somewhere dealing with him and his shenanigans.

Thanks to Luce's fondness for letting her mouth run away with her no matter who was listening, Jackson had picked up all kinds of things over the years. Things Sydney would never tell him. That she and her sister had different fathers and had been raised haphazardly by their mother, who had seemed determined to give them as unorthodox a childhood as possible.

*Which,* Luce had told him once, *is one way of saying that Aunt Melody's got a few bats loose in the belfry and is plain reckless.*

The Christmas before he'd met Sydney, the whole Grey family had descended upon Jackson Hole, Wyoming, where Melody Grey—if that was the name she used—had thrown herself a 50th birthday party that she'd treated like a kind of dating game. She'd invited every single ex-lover of hers who would come and revisited each of them and their chemistry to see if maybe she'd overlooked a great love in there somewhere. And ended up settling down, to everyone's great surprise, with Sydney's sister's father.

Who was a biker. In the *Sons of Anarchy* vein, according to Luce, who had made a face that Jackson thought meant that Luce thought the man was hot.

Information he hadn't needed.

But any information there was on Sydney, he liked to hoard.

*The funny thing is that nobody expected it to last more than a minute or two,* Luce had told Jackson one night while having dinner with her surly, problematic teenage boys at FlintWorks. *As Devyn always says, her mother is no good at making decisions. But her father? When he makes a decision, it's set in stone forever.*

Yet all Jackson could think about was what that must have been like for Sydney. The younger daughter, by a man who no one in the Grey family had laid eyes on since his divorce from Melody. A man who certainly hadn't showed up to play *what if* games with his ex that Christmas.

And given how little anyone in the Grey family laid eyes on Sydney—Luce claimed they had running bets on how many times she'd bail on family events each year—Jackson had to wonder how often she saw her father.

*Aunt Melody calls herself a free spirit,* Luce had told him. *So no one saw* stone *appealing to her.*

*She's more of a lost soul,* Luce's mother had chimed in, while her husband, Melody's brother Ryan, had only rolled his eyes.

Jackson had wanted to ask if that was why Sydney's deepest and longest relationship was a job, but he was the guy serving the drinks and the food that night. He wasn't supposed to be paying attention to Grey family stories that Luce seemed to tell purely to rile up her parents and her kids.

But he'd spent a lot of time during the dark, cold stretches of Montana winters, one after the next in those months after Christmas when he didn't have Sydney's holiday appearance to look forward to, wondering what it must have been like to grow up that way.

His own childhood had been steady as a rock, if sad in places. He and his mother had lived in the same house with his grandparents and he'd been in school a year or so before it occurred to him that not having a father made him different from a lot of his classmates. Because he didn't just not have a father, he had no stories about him, either. There were no pictures. There was nothing. His mother and his grandparents never spoke about the man who must have assisted in the creation of Jackson.

When he pushed, because of course he'd pushed a time or two, he'd always gotten different variations of the same response. They didn't think it mattered. The man who'd fathered him wasn't in their life and never would be.

It was always made clear, as kindly as possible, that further questions were unwelcome.

It wasn't until his mother finally got sick from those cigarettes she refused to give up that his sorrowed grandfather sat him down. Grandpa had told him that his mother—a saint in her son's eyes, never anything but calm and quiet and kind—had not always been the model of a good, churchgoing woman that she had always been for Jackson. She'd had a wild phase. Grandma and Grandpa had lost track of her. She had followed her restlessness out of the small town in the hill country where she'd grown up, straight for the bright lights and dark shadows of the bigger cities.

That was where she'd gone and got herself into trouble with a man who'd laughed at her when she told him what happened, tossed her a couple hundred-dollar bills, and had never looked back.

*If you want to go look for your kin, we won't stop you,* his grandfather had told him in that same voice of goodness and gravel that had defined most of Jackson's childhood.

*But I will ask you to keep your poor mama forever on your heart,* his grandmother had joined in. *The woman she wants to be now, even while she's dying. The one who raised you. The woman who turned her back on sin and did her best to walk into the light.*

Jackson had started using his mama's maiden name as his surname there and then.

And it wasn't until years later that he had to wonder why his mother hadn't given him her name from the start. Maybe she'd intended the Flint name as more of a spotlight, guiding him on his way and teaching him what not to be—but that wasn't the kind of thing a man asked of his mother while she fought cancer so bravely all those years.

Eventually he took that Flint surname back, but when he did, it hadn't taken him long to discover that the man he shared it with had been bad news, particularly for any woman who happened across his path, whether he'd bothered to marry them or not.

What interested Jackson more than one more sorry excuse for a man were his brothers. But not because they were rich.

The fact was, though Jackson didn't like to advertise it, he wasn't hurting for money. He'd had to figure out how to pay for his mama's care, or leave that as one more burden for his grandparents to pick up and carry. But they'd already spent their lives taking care of his mother and him, so he'd figured he might as well see what he could make happen on his own.

He'd been recruited right off the football field on Friday night in his little Texas hometown, played pretty decent college ball, then had made that coveted jump to the pros.

Where he'd played two seasons for an obscene amount of money and then quit while he was ahead. It was that or breaking every damn bone in his body beyond repair, and he'd known he wasn't good enough to risk that.

When he quit, he stopped using his mama's maiden name so it would be harder to be recognized by fans. That was when he'd gotten serious about hunting down what family he had on his father's side and seeing if they were worth knowing.

He thought his mama would have loved that he'd gotten her parents up here, so they could all sit down together with Jasper and Jonah Flint, tell stories about Jackson's mother and theirs, and let all that grief go somewhere for a minute.

All of those things had taken up a lot of his time and energy for a while. Ranch work because it was everything that football wasn't, but then, he'd missed football a hell of a lot too in those early years. Then Jasper had brought his surprise half brother in on FlintWorks so Jasper could spend more time with his young and growing family while Chelsea got into local politics, and that had taken up Jackson's time too.

There were a whole lot of reasons he didn't have a lot of hookups here, he thought now, and some of them had to do with all the huge life changes he'd been handling over the past few years. But it was also because he liked Marietta. He liked small-town Montana. He liked knowing his neighbors and the people he passed on the street.

It reminded him of all the things his mama had taught him to love about their hometown, but better, because here there were no clueless schoolkids to tease him about not having the fathers they did.

And while he wasn't the kind of man that people recognized out of context too often, it was also true that Jackson never liked to trade on what little fame football had brought him. He told himself that must be the reason he'd turned down pretty much every offer of companionship that had come his way since he'd turned up in Montana.

All except one.

Sydney Campbell, who was here for a whole four-month season this time around.

Jackson had been an excellent high school football player, a good college football player, and a decent enough pro football player. But in all cases, what he'd excelled at was thinking at least three moves ahead.

It was just that with Sydney, there were a lot of moves to be had, and she had the brain for chess games far above his paygrade.

But this was different.

This was his chance.

And Sydney was the smartest woman Jackson had ever

met, not to mention the hottest, but he was determined. The kind of determined that made his last name more of a warning—though the kind of warning he knew she wouldn't heed.

He wasn't above using that, either.

When her shift was over, she disappeared into the back of the bar for a few minutes. When she came out again, she didn't even glance in his direction. But he could see the way her lips curved as she waved goodbye to her uncle and walked out into the night.

The same way she always did.

As if the whole town was watching.

Which it probably was.

Jackson took his time finishing his drink. Then he made his excuses, said his goodbyes, and followed her out. Sometimes she waited for him right outside the door. Other times she walked the few streets over to the train depot and he followed her that way, breathing in the sweet anticipation of a quiet Montana night and the heat he knew he had waiting for him.

The man who'd once stood in stadiums packed with thousands of screaming fans might not have understood who he was now, but Jackson didn't need him to. He understood. There was a pleasure in both lives. But the difference was, this life he had now didn't have a shelf life. This life was independent of the strength of his knees or the state of his body or how far he could throw a ball. This life got better the deeper he sank into it, and there was no end in sight.

He was glad he knew enough to treasure it the way he knew his mama would have, if she'd lived long enough to see it.

And there was only one way he could think to make it any better.

So he walked outside, pleased that it was still fairly warm this early in September. It would change fast. The mornings were already cold and the sun didn't get as high or burn as hot as it had the previous couple of giddy summer months. He let the heavy saloon door slam behind him, his mouth curving when he caught sight of her.

She moved with an intense sort of grace, and he would know her anywhere for her gait alone. And the way the streetlights caught her hair and made it gleam bright red instead of its usual more serene auburn, like the lights knew the truth about the real Sydney.

The one Jackson only really saw in bed.

He followed her as she headed across the street and over towards the Graff. He caught up to her, and liked it probably more than he should when Sydney fell into place beside him, matching her stride to his.

They didn't touch, but they didn't have to.

He could already feel that heat building inside of him, the way it always did. The moment they were alone it would explode. It was always like that the first time after months apart. It was always fire and fury, muffled laughter and halfhearted curses as they tried to strip themselves, and each other, on their way to the nearest bed.

Or any private place they could find. They weren't always picky.

The second time was always slower. Deeper. More intense. It went on and on, like all that heat and yearning, joy and delight, was new.

It was the part after that he liked best.

They were usually in his place. She was always ravenously hungry, and surprised by that, so he knew without having to ask that she wasn't a woman who worked on her figure. She was a woman who forgot to eat. He wished his mama was alive so he could tell her that such women really did exist. Mama would roll her eyes into the back of her head with that smoky laugh of hers and tell him what he already knew, that she would sooner forget to put her head on her own body than put food in it.

Someday he meant to tell Sydney that. Someday.

He liked to cook for this woman, like maybe if he fed her enough, it would turn into the sort of fairy tale where eating the magic food made her stay—but it hadn't yet.

Jackson made anything that struck his fancy, just to watch her eat. He was fascinated by the way she did things like hold her fork, or cross her legs beneath her, or lean forward when he spoke as if listening took the whole of her body. He liked the way she tied up all that gleaming dark red hair into a knot on the top of her head, and didn't seem to know that the reason he liked kiss her *just there*, to the right of the actual nape of her neck, was because she had three freckles arranged there like a target.

Sometimes, when her belly was full and her eyes got sleepy, they could sit together on his couch. He could pull her feet in his lap and she might just get lazy enough to tell him a little story or two. Never about the work she did. Never about anything that might let him inside who she was now.

Her stories were always about Marietta. About running wild in the mountains and roaming about in the fields. About jumping off the bridge in the middle of town to paddle in the river. About floating around in the creek on her uncle Jason's property, staring up at the sky for hours, until her eyelids felt sunburned too.

Those were the moments he treasured.

Those were the moments he hoarded, so he could bring them out when she was gone and polish them all like little gems.

He wanted more.

And so when they stopped outside the entrance to the Graff, looking proud and Victorian beautiful, he didn't let her pull him inside with her the way she wanted.

"We don't have to go in if you don't want to." She smiled, and the world shifted all around her the way it always did. He ought to get used to it, but he never did. "You know I like your place just fine."

But what Sydney didn't know about him—one of the great many things Sydney didn't know about him—was that he wasn't at all moveable when it came to decisions either, and he wasn't any sort of biker. He'd always been that way. He was happy to go along until he wasn't, and once he made up his mind, there was no changing it.

He felt it in him, like iron tonight.

That was how much he wanted this to change. That was how much he wanted to take this opportunity that he'd been thinking would never come.

Even if, looking at her in the gathering darkness all around them, he couldn't help but question that.

Because surely only a madman would walk away from Sydney Campbell, no matter his reasons.

Her head was tipped back, so his whole world was the soft plumpness of her lips, that intoxicating intelligence in her eyes, and the tiny, surprisingly lush little body of hers that she never made the slightest effort to pretty up at all.

The pageant queens wouldn't know what to do with her and he thought she'd probably like that, out here tonight in a T-shirt, jeans, and no makeup like she knew she didn't have to do a damned thing but breathe to make him ache. Everywhere.

The thing was, he was a goner when it came to this girl and he had been from the start.

If he didn't do something to change this, it never would change. She would carry on just like this forever.

But he wanted a different kind of forever.

"I can come up or we can go to my place, sure," he said, and his voice sounded rougher than it should, because he knew he was taking a risk. Then again, he was Jackson Flint. Taking risks was what he did, and well. "But we won't be having sex, Sydney. Just so we're clear. We have some talking to do, you and me."

# Chapter Three

SYDNEY WAS SURE she couldn't have heard him right.

"What do you mean?" she asked.

His eyes were still that dark green, and still as hot as ever. She could *feel* the way he looked at her, and she knew what that meant. She would have said she could read him without even trying hard.

But Jackson only gazed down at her, out here in the dark, and he didn't relent. "Exactly what I said, darlin'."

She... didn't like that at all. And now she had to process not just what he'd said, but all the potential meanings and possibilities and complications, spinning all around them in the air when she'd thought this was all straightforward.

Because it had always been straightforward. Easy. *Right,* something in her suggested, but she brushed that aside.

Something was kicking in her, unpleasantly. Sydney was forced to face the fact that of all the things she was usually so good at had seemed to fail her entirely here. She hadn't picked up any clues that things were different now. She had no idea why he'd said something so out of left field, what he could possibly mean by it, or why he would have the slightest desire to change the way things always were between them.

Her heart was pounding in her chest. Her throat felt dry. It felt a lot like panic, and she didn't panic. She hadn't since she was a kid. It was the strangest, most unexpected physical reaction to something that hadn't occurred in as long she could remember—that being, that she, Sydney Campbell, didn't know something and couldn't figure it out.

If he'd punched her in the stomach she would have liked that a lot more.

Though it felt about the same.

"I don't understand," she managed to say, and it was a fight to make her voice sound… normal. Not thick with all that panic that shouldn't be there. Sydney told herself it was because she hadn't seen this coming, that was all. "You don't want…" *Me*, she almost said, but caught herself just in time. That was much too raw. Much too dangerous. "You don't want to have sex with me anymore?"

A storm crashed through his eyes then, but that wasn't any better. She couldn't identify that, either. She could see that it was happening, but it was like the reaction inside her—something mysterious and overwhelming that she couldn't quite read.

She didn't like this, either.

He took a moment, but it only made him look fiercer. "I don't think there will ever come a day on this earth that I won't want to have sex with you, Sydney. I'm not wired that way."

Her mouth was too dry. Her stomach hurt.

When she was a kid, the panic had wrecked her. Regularly. She'd felt faint. She'd had to try to breathe through it, telling herself she wasn't *actually* dying, no matter how it *felt*. She'd worked overtime to hide it, and she had, but she'd forgotten all her coping mechanisms. It had been years.

*Years*, she reminded herself. That was the thing to hold on to. She wasn't that little girl any longer, forever at the whims of the impossible adults in her life. She *was* the adult in her life now. And she could fall back on the tricks that had made her so great at her job. She could start at the beginning and work her way through everything all over again, the way she did when she wasn't finding the connections she wanted.

There was no reason a whole grown man couldn't be the same as a set of data points, she told herself. It was all in how you looked at things.

Even thinking about Jackson Flint that way, and this situation that way, made her feel calmer. Immediately.

Another reason she loved her job.

She frowned up at him. "It's not that you don't want to have sex." *With me.* But that wasn't helpful. She pushed on. "It's that you don't want to have sex *right now*. You want to… *talk*."

Sydney didn't actually make a face when she said that last word. She didn't think she did, anyway.

Still, Jackson looked almost amused. "That's what I said."

She nodded intelligently, the way she did in all her meetings. Because everyone was always competing to know the most in the world she inhabited, especially when asking questions. "What do you want to talk about?"

"Is this where you want to have that conversation?"

And that was when she really paid attention to where they were. There weren't tons of people around. This was Marietta, not DC. But still, they were standing out in the open, right there by the front entrance to the Graff. Anyone could see them.

Was that what the problem was? He didn't want anyone to see him with her? She had always thought that she was the one who was keeping things private, because she kept everything private. Especially where her family was involved—and for her, her family and Marietta had always been the same thing.

"Are you married?" she asked him. A little flatly. Maybe a little aggressively.

Maybe more than a little.

But even Sydney couldn't pretend she didn't feel something—a whole lot of something—when Jackson threw back his head and laughed. It was all those splendid, artistic lines of his absurdly beautiful body, in jeans and a T-shirt and a cowboy hat. It was the sheer abandon on his face. As if he could laugh forever, just him and the Montana sky and that laugh that made all the twisty, panicky things in her hum a little.

As if, when she wasn't around, he laughed all the time.

Sydney told herself that there was absolutely no reason that notion should land on her like a knife sunk deep. There was no reason she should hurt over things she'd made up in her head. Over how this man *laughed.*

Or the way it felt like peace and joy inside her, when it was nowhere near Christmas and anyway, Grey family gatherings were more about obligatory appearances and too much whiskey than any glad tidings.

"I'm not married," Jackson said, and he shook his head a little, like he couldn't believe she'd asked him that. "But that's part of what I'd like to talk to you about."

Her heart did something that had to be the precursor to a cardiac event, and the end of her. "Marriage?"

"Okay," he said, as if she'd answered a question instead of asked one. "If you don't want to be civilized, that's fine. Come with me."

He turned and walked away from the front entrance of the Graff, leaving her with no choice but to either stand there staring after him, or follow him.

Well. She could always turn around, walk inside, and go handle all this panic alone in her hotel room without getting any answers.

But somehow that was not all appealing.

And not only because Sydney knew perfectly well that without concrete answers and verifiable facts, she spiraled around and around, making up things in her head and reacting to them like they were true. Or she had, way back before she'd very deliberately made herself a life that cut down on even the urge to ask questions that she couldn't find the answers for, all by herself. And fast.

So, grudgingly, she followed him.

She left the lights that lit up the front of the Graff, trailing after Jackson and that saunter of his. She followed him, telling herself this was a fact-finding mission and nothing more, no need to panic her way into an embarrassing hospital visit that her family would definitely think was a sign of her *condition*. But she was worrying at her fingernails when he led her to a bench that was set back off Main Street in front of the small church.

Sydney couldn't believe that he really meant to just… *sit there*. On a *bench*. This late in the evening when there were so many other things they could be doing—

But he did.

And then Jackson gazed at her, a kind of mild challenge all over him, and she couldn't think of anything to do but walk over and sit down next to him.

Though she made sure to look annoyed by the whole thing.

"Have you spent your fair share of time sitting on a pretty bench on a pretty night?" he asked, and really, it wasn't fair. That drawl of his was a weapon. She had always preferred minimize the damage it could do by occupying his mouth in other ways, and that might have been a mistake.

Because now it danced over her like a whole new set of stars.

"Oh, sure," Sydney muttered. "If by a pretty bench you mean at my desk, and by a pretty evening you mean in my office. Yeah. I sit there all the time."

He didn't quite sigh, but it almost felt as if he did. She had no idea why she found herself suddenly wrapping her arms across her middle and curling them around herself like she needed a hug, of all things. Just like she had no idea why she was frowning as if she'd said something stupid. Or revealing.

Or both.

"How many dates do you go on, back in DC?" he asked, all friendly and conversational.

Sydney laughed, and though it wasn't quite the show of abandon he'd put on before, it felt close. Maybe tinged with a little more edge. *Or hysteria*, something in her suggested.

It didn't help that she knew she'd started them down this road, hadn't she? By asking if he was married. After all these years.

Meanwhile, they were sitting on a bench by a church beneath the stars, having a quiet little talk that made her feel like she was dying. Or she assumed that was what all this *stuff* in her was. Why not just answer him? What could it hurt? "Between you and me and Copper Mountain, I'm not sure that I've ever been on a date."

That had sounded funny in her head. Maybe even a little snarky.

But that wasn't how it landed with the man beside her,

who stretched his arm out along the back of the bench—though he still didn't touch her—and looked at her like those eyes of his could see straight through her. To all that panic and pressure inside.

"That's a crying shame," Jackson said, all heat and drawl.

Sydney was determined to make this light again. Easy. To get away from all this *nervousness*, or whatever this was. "I don't even understand what a date is," she continued. "Everyone's always doing it now. Swiping around on screens and then going out for *coffee*. It sounds hideous. Anybody can look good in a picture but that doesn't mean I want to have *coffee* with them."

"You do know that the purpose of going for coffee isn't the coffee, I hope." More of that dark green, *knowing* look. "It's the talking."

He sounded amused again and she didn't know why it got to her like that. Why it made her feel jumpy and vulnerable and *seen* when it shouldn't matter. This was Marietta. None of this should matter. She wasn't a person who let things matter to her.

But when she went to get up, she… didn't.

He seemed much too aware of her struggle. "The point of a date, Sydney, is that two people sit down and try to get to know each other. Feel each other out a little bit."

She was sure he did not mean the only kind of *feeling out* she was good at. And she was equally sure he knew exactly what she was thinking.

Jackson managed to look entertained and reproving at the same time. "It doesn't have to be all about childhood trauma, deep feelings, or even anything remotely important. The questions to ask are things like, does this person interest me? Can we have a conversation? Do we make each other laugh? Is there any possibility that at any time in this life, I might want to take off all my clothes and all of this person's to see what might happen?" Before she could make a comment on that, he kept going. "And more important, if I do, will I want to look this person full in the face come morning?"

They had never had a morning. Sydney knew that was for any number of perfectly rational reasons. There was always someone's house to sneak back into. There were family members who would notice if she stayed out. It had nothing to do with worrying that if she saw a sunrise with this man, she'd… lose herself completely, turn into her mother, and try to move in with him or something.

*Not to mention, you think that if you keep this nothing but a series of random hookups, it will never mean anything,* an annoying voice inside her pronounced.

She felt breathless, then, and off-balance. That annoyed her, so she glared at him. But glaring didn't make it better, because he was close beside her and all around her and *not touching her.*

Worse, he was looking straight at her, too much heat and smoke in his gaze.

"Is this your way of telling me that you go on lots of dates?" she asked, reluctantly, because she didn't want to know. She liked the Jackson in her head. She liked the Jackson who she kept close in the few nights she was alone and at home and not neck-deep in some crisis. She wasn't sure she wanted to know the details that made him real.

She wasn't sure she liked *real.* In her experience, *real* had claws and left to its own devices, left scars.

"I haven't dated in some time," Jackson said, and it all felt… significant. The sort of thing she would flag if she found it, then pass on to her colleagues like some sort of map. "Doesn't sound like you have either."

"I haven't done anything that would classify as an actual date," she said, though her ribs were starting to hurt. Possibly straining against all that *significance.* Or aiming her toward the hospital, like it or not. "I said that already."

Jackson ran a hand over his face. He took his cowboy hat off and laid it beside him on the bench and ran his fingers through his hair, too. He didn't *actually* sigh. He just embodied a sigh.

And then he fixed her with all that smokey, dark green attention once again. "What I'm trying to ascertain, Sydney, is whether or not you get naked with other people in between the times that you get naked with me."

There it was. Reality. Significance.

A wound like a scar in its infancy, marking her right there where she sat.

Sydney felt her breath catch. And there was surely no reason for her heart to start pounding like that again. There was no reason that her stomach should knot up the way it did. She understood that heavy softness between her legs. She understood why she could feel the fabric of the clothes she wore rubbing against every bit of her skin, agitating her, making her want to take them off and wear him instead.

But what she didn't understand was why talking to this man, who she'd seen naked more times than she should count, should feel as if she was stripping down before him at last. And once she did, well.

Then he would *see*. Then he would *know*.

Everything *caught* in her. Again. And worse this time.

If Sydney wanted to be seen like that, she would probably live a life that took place outside her cave of an office. If Sydney wanted to be *seen*, she would spend more time with people she'd known all her life. If she wanted to be *seen* she wouldn't be here, with him.

This was not the purpose of Marietta. Not for her.

She went with the rush of outrage. It felt cleaner. "Are you asking for a *count*? A tally? Is that really what we're going to do here?"

"It's less a question about numbers and more a question about intentions, darlin', but I expect you know that."

The way he looked at her hurt. Or maybe she just hurt. Maybe this was the jet lag she never usually suffered from, setting in hard.

"I thought we were tacitly agreeing not to ask what happens in between these nights. I like that tacit agreement. Why don't we go back to that?" But she could hear too much in her own voice. That panic. That uncertainty.

That vulnerability, damn him.

Jackson looked almost gentle, and that was worse. "Sydney."

Maybe she wouldn't have said anything, because why should she say anything, but he was looking at her. He was *looking* at her the way he always did. As if he could see straight into the heart of her. Her own family complained that she was too closed off, too private, but Jackson never seemed to notice.

Maybe if she'd been smart enough to look away she could have kept her barriers nice and high.

"I can't remember the last time I was with somebody other than you," she muttered, ungraciously.

And that was true, but she'd never thought about it like that before. She'd certainly never stated it so baldly. Not even to herself. As she sat here on this bench in the open night air that she knew perfectly well wasn't spinning around and around and around, she felt dizzy all the same. Kind of seasick, really.

Because she hadn't, in all these years of thinking about Jackson like he was some kind of *location*—the only vacation she allowed herself—ever let herself think about that one, telling little detail.

She wasn't sure she wanted to think about it now.

It wasn't as if she'd gone out on the prowl a whole lot before Jackson. There was always a lot of time in between—like years—and such adventures always followed the same script. She would find herself staring at the ceiling in her strange, ill-fitting apartment. She would get to thinking that there had to be better things she could be doing with her time on the few nights she was lying in a bed at all. So she would go out. She would find a bar, have a few shots, and let men hit on her.

Sometimes that was enough. Sydney got to feel like a normal girl for a while, not a walking amalgamation of data points, rumors, and highly classified speculation. Sometimes she would flirt a little, drink a little more, then put herself in a taxi back home.

Every once in a while, someone was a little more appealing than the usual mess of them, so she'd go home with them instead.

But she couldn't remember the last time she'd done anything like that. Or even wanted to do anything like that. She didn't even let men hit on her any more. It was all just… wrong.

*Not Jackson,* that little voice supplied, so helpfully.

Sydney knew then that if she really focused, the way she hadn't done in some five-odd years, she would discover that she hadn't done any of these things since before she'd met Jackson. Since that Christmas she'd spent in Jackson Hole, not only watching her mother actually fall in love again—which wasn't new or interesting—but watching her sister do the same.

When Devyn had always been Sydney's touchstone. She and Devyn were the only ones who knew exactly what it was like to grow up in Melody Grey's chaotic wake. Devyn was the only one Sydney could be honest with about all of that, because they'd been in it together.

If Devyn could fall in love, what did it mean that Sydney couldn't?

What was *wrong* with her?

Then a year later, she'd run into Jackson at Grey's and one of the best things about *that* was the way he'd made her feel… new.

Normal, maybe.

She'd felt like the kind of girl who could scratch an itch, revel in the kind of delicious sex they had as if it could go on forever, and then not get weird about it after. Wasn't that the gold standard that everyone was supposed to aspire to?

Sydney had been so sure that she'd had that, at last, that there was no more need to beat herself up about what she could or couldn't feel.

And she didn't realize that she'd lapsed off into her own head until she felt his fingers on her chin. He tipped her head up and toward him, so she had no choice but to look straight at him again.

Not like that was a hardship. The man got better-looking

every time she saw him.

But his hands were on her, and that always changed things. She could feel him everywhere. Like a song she could only sing when he was near. Brighter and wilder than any song she'd ever known.

"I haven't touched anybody else either," he told her, with a kind of solemnity that shivered through her. It, too, felt *significant* in ways she told herself she wanted to avoid. "Not in five years. And I've never been much of a monk before, Sydney."

She tugged her chin out of his grasp. "I don't know what you want me to say to that."

"I don't recall asking you to say anything."

He looked so calm, was the thing. So completely and utterly at ease. Meanwhile, she was sure that he could see that she was sweating a little bit. Maybe he could even hear the way her heart was clattering around against her ribs. It was a nightmare.

"I'm going to ask you a question," Jackson said then. "And I don't want a knee-jerk answer. Do you understand? I don't want you to answer without thinking it through."

"I know what knee-jerk means."

His lips curved, but he kept going. "You have four months here in town this time. What would happen if we didn't do this the same way we always do it?"

"So you really, actually, don't want to have sex with me."

"You understand what knee-jerk means, but that doesn't

prevent you from jerking that knee, is that it?"

Sydney flushed at that, but shut her mouth.

Jackson sat back. His Stetson was still on the bench beside him, and he looked like the sort of cowboy sculpture a town like this would commission at some point or another. He was that rugged. That beautiful. And when he looked off into the distance, he made her feel the way she did every time she got a look at the Rockies again.

Like she was soaring, even if her feet were planted firmly on the ground.

He took his time looking at her, and she thought she felt his fingers in her hair, though it could have been the faint little breeze that meandered along. "What if we dated?"

That word sat there between them, stark. Strange.

Sydney's head spun, but all she could think was that if he hadn't wanted to have this strange and uncomfortable conversation, if he hadn't insisted on it, they would already be naked. He would already be deep inside of her, filling her up and making her arch into him, the only time she ever felt that kind of abandon she'd seen in him when he laughed.

Peace and joy and light and *him.*

She accepted the fact that she was deeply resentful it was not happening. Right now.

So she scowled at him, and that felt as close to good as she figured she'd be getting tonight. "I'm not sure what part of this conversation made you think that dating was something that appealed to me."

"I think we should date," Jackson said, a lot like he hadn't heard her. Or was, in fact, actively ignoring her. "I feel like we're doing things backwards. Here's our chance to set that ship right."

"It's not a ship. It's… mutually beneficial…" There was a word she could have used, but she couldn't bring herself to say it. Not when he was right here, *looking* at her.

Because he was the only person alive who not only knew every detail of what had happened between them, but would also know better if she used a dismissive word to describe it. She also had the skittery sort of notion that he wouldn't react well to her attempts to minimize it, either.

Jackson gazed at her as if he knew full well what she was thinking. Which he did way too much of. "You're not sleeping with anyone else. I'm not either." She decided she hated how patient he sounded. How irritatingly *calm*. Like she was some wild horse he could tame with a soft, steady voice. "What if I told you that dating me was the only way you and I will be sleeping together again?"

Sydney felt suspiciously like that wild horse she'd just been thinking about, and she didn't like it. "I would say that in addition to being not at all what I want, that also sounds suspiciously like an ultimatum."

"Are we in a relationship? Can we make ultimatums?"

She glared at him. "You're trying to manipulate me into dating you."

"Call it what you want," Jackson shot back. "I'm making

a stand." He leaned a little bit closer, and she suddenly found it hard to breathe. "Access to my body comes with conditions now. I'm not manipulating you into that. I'm stating a fact. You can do with that fact what you like."

She wanted to argue. She wanted to do a lot more than argue—she wanted to throw a Melody-style fit, mostly as an excuse to get her hands on him. Then they'd see what kind of conditions he thought he could hold himself to.

But even though she could envision too easily how exactly to go about doing that, she didn't.

Because throwing a fit like that, even in her own mind's eye, looked a little too much like someone who cared.

A lot.

"Lay out your conditions," she bit out instead, and crossed her arms like they'd suddenly found themselves at a negotiating table.

"I don't intend to cut you off entirely," Jackson drawled.

"Out of the goodness of your heart, of course."

"And also because it's not easy for me to be near you and not inside you." And he made sure he was looking at her while he said that. "In case you wondered."

She felt herself glow with the heat of that. "I did wonder, actually. As I think I mentioned, without a single jerky knee."

"There's no hooking up in bars," he said sternly, though his eyes gleamed. And maybe she'd leaned in a little herself, now that she thought about it. "We'll go on a date. That date will include talking. I already know what you look like naked, Sydney. Praise God. Now I want to get to know *you*."

Her throat was so dry she was surprised it didn't spark a fire right there and then. She tried to swallow. Once, again.

Then she gave up. "And what if I told you that you're setting yourself a fool's errand with that?"

Jackson only shook his head, though there was something softer in the way he looked at her. She had to look away. "If that's meant to be a deterrent, it's not working."

"Do you want me to compile a depressing biography?" she demanded, glaring straight ahead at the church now. "Do you want me to make a bullet-pointed list of all my childhood trauma? What will you consider enough unfortunate information to just… get back to the good stuff?"

"Sydney," he said quietly. "Baby. It's all you. That is the good stuff."

He reached over and took her hand, lacing his fingers in hers. And she had taken this man inside her body more times than she could count. She had learned every inch of his skin and had fallen asleep in his arms, wrecked so beautifully it could still make her shiver.

And still nothing made her heart jolt as when he lifted her knuckles to his lips and brushed a kiss there. "I know you don't believe me, but you'll see. All you have to do is trust me."

Sydney didn't know how to tell him that trust was something she couldn't do. Ever.

Or how to tell herself that here, now, with Jackson so close to her and the Montana night pressing in like its own sweet heat, she actually wished she could.

But then, to her astonishment, he stood up and pulled her with him. And then he walked her back to the front of the Graff, where he actually let go of her hand and stepped back.

"You're not coming in," she said, in disbelief.

Jackson shook his head. "You know the rules."

She turned toward the front door, but she didn't move. Maybe she couldn't. "And what if I can't play this game with you?" she asked, though it cost her. "What if I'm not who you think I am?"

"I know who you are, Sydney. I'm not worried about that at all."

And she shook, when it wasn't even cold. She looked back over her shoulder. "I don't know if I can do this."

He didn't close the distance between them. He only gazed at her, something fierce and uncompromising on his beautiful face, and that was worse.

Much worse.

"You can," he told her, like he already knew. Like it was inevitable. "And when you're ready, you can come find me."

And then, while she watched in a dazed kind of amazement, not sure what she felt but aware it was *too much*—

Jackson turned and left her there.

Alone.

# Chapter Four

SYDNEY DID NOT enjoy staring up at the ceiling in her hotel room of the Graff in the least, no matter that it had fine moldings, and many other lovely period details that made it more interesting than the ceiling in her little apartment back east.

That was not exactly a high bar.

She finally fell asleep sometime around dawn, only to wake up later feeling out of sorts and hung over, when she hadn't been anything even approaching that kind of drunk.

Maybe it would have been better if she had been. If she'd been silly with it. She could pretend she didn't remember… anything.

But that would be childish, she told herself virtuously.

She dragged herself out of bed, and instead of opening her email and checking her texts obsessively the way she did every morning back home, she reminded herself—the way she had yesterday—that she was on holiday. And yes, it was looking less holiday-ish than it had before.

But it was still a holiday, like it or not.

However she looked at it and however it felt, the reality was that she had four months to do… whatever she wanted.

And not, this time, as a kid Melody had dumped her here for a summer. But as a grown woman who had chosen to come here, because she liked this town. She liked Montana.

Sometimes a good daydream about Montana was the only thing that got her through a bad day at work.

*And by Montana,* that voice in her chimed in, a little too smugly, *I think we know you mean Jackson.*

Sydney stretched. She told the voice inside her to shut up. Then she stood in the middle of her decidedly old west suite, with a view over Marietta and Copper Mountain rising high in the distance, and decided it was high time she built herself a new life.

Or at least, a vacation sort of life that could hold her the next four months.

One that was completely different from the one she'd been living.

"The good news is, that won't be hard," she muttered to herself, then went into the bathroom to splash water on her face and think about trying on new lives.

When she'd pulled on some clothes she went downstairs, taking a few moments to look around in awe at the old time splendor of the place. No expense had been spared, that was clear, and it made her feel like she was time traveling.

Sydney made her way outside, following old memories and an even older map in her head until she found a coffee place. She made herself smile and chat a little with the barista—if they called them baristas here—because that was what small-town people were like. They saw fewer people every day, so they could be nicer to them. City people were too busy protecting their space from the endless incursions on it by strangers to risk being randomly nice.

Then she took a lazy walk around Marietta while she drank her coffee—strong and bitter, the way she liked it, looking at the pretty houses on Bramble Lane before looping back in front of the courthouse. She noticed all the signs for the coming rodeo, and confronted the fact that despite her deep, deep roots out here in the country, she had never been to a rodeo.

And she'd never been *here* for *this* rodeo, either. Though if the signs she saw were right, it was also the weekend of her grandparents' 70th anniversary. No one was going to say it out loud, least of all Sydney, but it would likely be their last. They were so old now. So frail.

They were both the same as they'd always been, mentally—meaning they were both feisty and happy to argue over every last thing—but then, they'd never called themselves a love match. Quite the opposite. Elly liked to make it sound as if she'd sacrificed herself to her marriage like some kind of longsuffering vestal virgin.

*You make it all sound so appealing,* Melody had said once, dry enough that it was tempting to think that was the real her. Not all that ditzy, selfish nonsense she called *following her bliss.*

*It's not,* Elly had snapped back. *Marriage is torture. It's about how you survive it in the face of all its hardships.*

*Thanks,* her then-surly cousin Jesse had drawled over the Thanksgiving table that year. *I think I'll take up ultra-running with an Ironman or two to spice it up. Sounds less grueling.*

Sydney smiled at the memory, but now it had her wondering. Could the rodeo have actually brought her grandparents together? Did they have a sweet little country song origin story they'd been keeping to themselves?

According to her mother, that sort of thing was impossible. She had always maintained that her parents' marriage had been built on spite, shame, and straight up martyrdom.

Sydney had never wanted to point out to her mother that at least her grandparents had provided some kind of foundation, happy or not. Melody certainly couldn't say the same about any of her attempts at marriage, including the five years she'd spent actually wedded to Sydney's father.

But that was family, wasn't it? Nostalgia when you weren't with them, and then a whole lot of biting your tongue when you were.

It had been six years ago in Jackson Hole, when Melody had been putting on her most bonkers performance yet, that Sydney had admitted to Devyn at last that she had not exactly had a supportive and stable existence in her dad's house no matter how she might have presented it at the time. Because Stanley Campbell had made no secret of the fact he viewed her as the walking, talking mistake he'd made with Melody—when he was a man who otherwise never made mistakes.

He'd never let Sydney forget it.

But he was also meticulous to a fault, so he'd never missed a single moment of the time allotted him in the custody agreement he'd worked out with Melody. He had dutifully picked Sydney up, kept her the requisite amount of time, and let her work out for herself that he treated his children with his new wife a whole lot better than he'd ever treated her.

She'd tried to pretend otherwise for a long time.

Once she'd admitted it to Devyn, though, it shifted something inside her. She felt… free, in a way. She no longer felt the need to try to prove herself to someone who would never, ever see her or care about her at all.

It was better to feel alone while actually being alone than to sit at her father's table in Baltimore with the kids he actually loved and feel like she didn't exist.

When she was alone, she didn't have to feel a thing.

She *liked* not feeling. Feeling things sucked, and in case she wanted to waver on that, there was last night to prove it.

Sydney took a pull of her coffee and decided she could do that here in Marietta, too. Hell, she was good at it.

After all, she had family here, and family was often a great way to feel alone while in large groups. Or, better yet, she could act like the cartoon version of Sydney that they'd developed over the years and treated as the real her, no need to dive in any deeper.

She liked that, too, even if her family was much different

than they'd used to be now. Entirely too many of them were distressingly happy these days. They'd used to tell each other the tale of the great family curse. Their grandmother had always made dark intimations that their grandfather's wild ways were an inherited trait, and they would all be miserable forever because of it.

Maybe because all of her children, save one, had pretty much proven that to be the case.

Sydney and her cousins had laughed about the Grey Curse in their teens, referenced it ironically as they got older, and then started worrying about it a whole lot more as they grew older still.

Currently in her thirties, Sydney couldn't say she was *worried* about it. Not really. It was more that she'd surrendered herself to the Grey Curse long ago. She'd been under the impression that everyone else had, too.

But instead, almost all of her cousins had actually broken the curse. Well. Except Uncle Jason's daughters—out of the three, only Rayanne ever came home, and only rarely—and Luce, who like to talk about the beauty of divorce in the speeches she couldn't be kept from giving at weddings. These days there was a whole new generation of first cousins once removed, and family gatherings had changed from everyone drinking in corners and hiding from their grandmother's wrath to, well, all of that but with little kids running all around, and brightening up the mood, like it or not.

Sometimes Sydney felt like if she wasn't careful, she

would *become* her grandmother.

And she couldn't said why, today, that seemed like the worst Grey Curse yet.

She looped around again and wandered up Main Street proper this time, charmed the way she always was. Marietta was pretty and gleaming in the warm morning sun. There were flower baskets overflowing with happy, colorful blooms. Flags waved and there was even bunting strewn about, making it all seem more festive than usual.

Some of the storefronts were different than she remembered, because she was always comparing the town before her to the pictures of it she kept tucked away in her memory. But no matter how much time passed, there were parts that were always the same. Not just Grey's Saloon, an institution at this point, if she said so herself.

But there was something about a Western frontier town, even if the frontier had moved on long ago. There was something about a place that was built entirely around people's desire for something, anything better. That was what had brought people here. That was why her own family had left the east, trusting blindly there had to be something over the horizon that was better than what little they had there.

Not that Sydney related to that notion at all.

*She* was on vacation.

The pretty mountains rising all around helped with that. Vacations were meant to be taken in beautiful places, and the glory of the Rocky Mountains definitely qualified. Old Copper Mountain itself, looming over the town, was a monument to dreams and dreams denied at once, and that was a good thing.

It did not make her think of curses and legends, much less family legacies.

*Her* family had opted out of that brutal mining life. They'd sidestepped it entirely.

Maybe that was the true Grey Curse. All that sidestepping and before you knew it, your descendant was standing in a town you helped build with blood and sweat and too many tears, calling it a vacation.

And she told herself there was no reason at all something should snake through her at that, like a little tickle, as if urging her to look more closely at things than she wanted to. She was *on vacation*, she reminded herself. She would be looking into nothing except the nearest spa, and possibly designer drinks that she could prepare at Grey's for the singular purpose of horrifying her uncle.

She wandered back over to the hotel, but instead of heading straight for her room, she stayed in the lobby, found a place to sit, and then let herself do nothing at all but soak in the atmosphere.

The way people on vacation did.

*God,* she thought. *Vacations are boring.*

"There you are," came a familiar voice.

Sydney wasn't sure she'd ever been *quite* so happy to see

her cousin Luce. Her older cousin bounded toward her, looking the way she always did—like a temper tantrum dressed for a hike. She wrapped Sydney up in a big hug, complete with an extra squeeze and that *humming* thing people did.

Sydney was not a hugger. Or a hummer.

But she made no move to pull away from her cousin.

"I can't believe you've been here long enough to piss off our grandparents *and* get Uncle Jason to give you a job and you haven't even come over to say hi," Luce was saying as they finally broke apart. "I should be insulted. But this is what happens when you raise three boys, Sydney. You lose the ability to get wound up about things. I can see the look on your face. You think I'm wound up as it is. What I'm telling you is that if it weren't for my kids, I would be dangerous."

Sydney laughed, and sat back down. Luce tossed herself into the antique armchair that sat on a diagonal to her without the slightest indication that she knew that it was breakable and valuable.

"I knew I'd see you sooner or later," Sydney said. "This is Marietta, not DC. You can't actually avoid people here."

She hoped that wasn't true. Because if it was, she was going to have an awkward time avoiding Jackson for the next four months.

And she fully intended to avoid Jackson and his dating game forevermore, thank you.

Luce was still talking, but then, Luce was always talking. "I would offer you the guest room again, but I don't blame you. I wouldn't stay at my house either. They're a bunch of animals."

But she smiled as she said it, settling in her armchair, and looking the way Luce always looked. Less aggrieved than during the harder years of her divorce, maybe. But still one hundred percent Luce. Crackling with that energy of hers, like she might burst up at any moment to do something athletic, like hike to the top of Copper Mountain. Or whip up a huge meal that could feed all her boys and all their friends.

She wasn't jittery, but still. She was a doer. Not a sitter.

They were the most diametrically opposed cousins in the family, Sydney had often thought. *She* was not a doer. She was a brain in a jar. She was paid for it.

"What do you think about the Grey Curse?" Sydney asked.

"I am the Grey Curse," Luce said at once. "Why did I ever marry that idiot? I can't answer that. Well. I can. He was the best I'd ever had, by which I mean the only, and I was a dumb teenager. Joke's on me, I guess."

"You can find someone else," Sydney said, aware that she sounded slightly more intense than she would have, say, yesterday. Before sitting on a bench with Jackson Flint, *talking*. "That's allowed, you know."

"The question I have to ask myself, Sydney, is why

would I want to train up some man?" Luce made a face. "I've spent the last nineteen years trying to housetrain three boys. I don't need to add a man to the mix. They're more trouble than they're worth."

"What if one came fully trained?"

Luce's eyes glinted. "I'd be more likely to believe in Bigfoot." She studied Sydney. "Why? Don't tell me you're about to move from the cursed column to the charmed life. We're some of the only remaining members of the family loveless club."

Sydney laughed. "I'm immune to love in any form, don't you worry."

"Are you sure?" Her cousin smiled. "I received no fewer than five phone calls, okay, they were texts, informing me that someone who looks a whole lot like my cousin was seen gallivanting about with Jackson Flint in the middle of the night last night."

"There were not five people anywhere near that park bench," Sydney said calmly, because acting like something was no big deal and she was surprised to hear that anyone cared was, always, an excellent first defense. "I question your sources."

"But the report was true, all the same?"

Sydney smiled. "You know that I know Jackson, Luce."

"I have suspicions about the nature of how you know Jackson, sure," Luce agreed. "But as Biblical as I imagine it is, I didn't think it ran to cuddling up near churches."

Sydney cautioned herself not to grip her coffee too hard between her palms, because it was coffee, not one of the rubber stress balls she liked to grip at work. If she kept it up, she would spill what was left of her coffee all over herself, and worse, she would give Luce that much more to gossip about.

"Did you come here to interrogate me?" she asked lightly. "Chastise me for breaking curfew? Do I have a curfew?"

"There's no curfew," her cousin said merrily. "But Marietta *is* a small town. In the end, they really come to the same thing."

"There was no *cuddling*," Sydney said, shaking her head. "I can assure you of that."

And that wasn't even a lie. Because *cuddling* wasn't a word that she would use, ever. Also, they hadn't touched that much. And his desire to *date* wasn't the same thing at all.

"I am personally dead inside and plan to remain so evermore," Luce said, with a wave of her hand. "But even I am alive enough to notice that Jackson Flint is smoking hot."

"No one said that he wasn't smoking hot. I said there was no *cuddling*. On a bench or otherwise."

Luce laughed at that, and then she shifted in her chair, which was punctuation where she was concerned. She sat straighter.

"So I've been thinking," she said.

"God help us."

Luce ignored that. "We're the only ones here in town.

Christina is just over the mountains, but she has her hands full with all the babies. I also have my hands full, but I'm always trying to get away from *my* babies. Anyway, I'm thinking we need to do something for Grandma and Grandpa's anniversary."

"Like a cake?" When Luce sighed, Sydney laughed. "I'm not sure surprises are a good idea. They're old. Very old."

"Grandma's too mean to die. And Grandpa is made entirely of whiskey and lies. I think they're going to live forever, and we should plan something to celebrate them, even if they hate it."

"I was wondering about the timing," Sydney found herself saying. "I never put it together that they got married during the rodeo."

And as she said it, she felt that little kick inside her. Maybe it was a spark. She didn't know what to call it, because sometimes it wasn't there at all, and then other times it lit up just like now—and that was how she made the connections she did. She followed that little bit of kindling to see where it went.

And for some reason, she felt it now. Even though she'd grown up listening to her grandmother tell stories of her history and her grandfather, all of it negative.

"Interesting." Luce looked almost entertained. "Imagine if there was some secret romantic story there? Nothing would scandalize me more. But even if there was, it was seventy years ago. I don't know how we figure out what really happened. There are only so many people in their nineties shuffling about."

"That part is all me," Sydney said, with a grin. "If there's something to find I can assure you, I'll find it."

And that was how she found herself in the local library with her laptop at the ready, otherwise known as Sydney Campbell at her happiest.

Better yet, as she dug into the local history of Marietta to see if she could find out more about the tales her grandparents didn't tell them, she barely thought about Jackson at all.

That's what she kept telling herself.

*Just watch,* she told him at night, staring triumphantly at her ceiling. *I can do this forever.*

# Chapter Five

JACKSON KNEW THAT Sydney was stubborn. Hell, he wouldn't like her as much if she wasn't. Still, he could admit to himself that he'd expected her to come to him sooner.

The next night, even.

When she didn't, when one day turned into yet another long night—except this time with the full knowledge that she was right here in Montana instead of across the country—he found himself second-guessing this stand he decided to make. Hard.

He found himself wondering what the big deal was.

And he was definitely questioning his own sanity for turning her down. Because what kind of fool turned down a woman like Sydney? What was he thinking?

He didn't have to look in his mirror to know the answer. He felt it in him, like a virus that wouldn't let go. Like the aches and pains that foretold a coming disaster. Like he was about to get very, very ill.

But he didn't.

Because no one had ever said that determination was easy. No one had ever suggested that it was fun to stand your ground and speak up for the things you actually wanted.

In point of fact, Jackson couldn't think of a single time in his life that it hadn't sucked.

But he still thought he knew Sydney pretty well, despite how little she seemed to want that. And how very little she'd given him to go on. He'd picked up every clue and then pored over each one. What she did with her beloved data, he did with her. He studied her the way he'd used to study football plays, his opponents, and every possible outcome to any potential choice.

And he wasn't sure he was three moves ahead when it came to this woman, though the conversation they'd had on that park bench made a lot of things he'd only hoped were true… clear at last.

She didn't have a string of men stashed in various places, kicking around while waiting for her to show up on her infrequent visits. Jackson had never been *worried* about that, not really, but he'd thought about it. He'd spent more than one very long, very dark Montana winter thinking on exactly that, in detail.

But far as he could tell and had ever been able to tell, she really didn't have anything at all except her job, this town with all her family members who lived here and came here on holidays, and him.

Jackson had to figure he could work with that.

And one thing he knew as a man who had played games professionally at the highest level, and then as a man who had faced off with Mother Nature and any number of ornery animals on the ranches around Paradise Valley, was that sometimes victory depended on knowing that the best offense, now and again, was standing still.

Waiting.

Letting them come to you.

It was no matter that really, he'd rather have bamboo shoved under his fingernails. Or any other form of torture. All of that would be better than this.

Waking up in the night, certain that any noise he heard was her, creeping in under cover of darkness. Unable to focus when he was in the brewery, tending to the paperwork and fielding calls all while reacting to every footstep in the hall, every sound of a door opening or closing, like it was finally going to be her.

Like she was going to come back to him just because he wanted her to.

By the middle of the week, he was heartily sick of himself.

But one of the good things about forcing this round of cold turkey on the both of them—and Jackson had to believe that it really was the *both* of them or he thought he might have a heart attack—was that there was no sense putting all of this willpower and suffering and mental gymnastics to waste. Every hour that passed without her showing up before him made him, if not happier with the situation in any way, then at least more resolved to continue.

Because he, by God, was not putting himself through this just to break now, get absolutely nothing he wanted—well, *almost* nothing that he wanted—and teach her that all she had to do was wait him out.

That was not the kind of thing he wanted her to learn.

Not from him.

He came to welcome the hours that the brewery was open, serving food while local bands played, because there was always something to do. And it was difficult to get his full brood on when he was more than likely jumping in to help out a server or otherwise getting hands-on with the inevitable catastrophes that cropped up in the course of a typical day. Besides, by now he knew most of the locals who showed up, and liked the opportunity to catch up with them. Summer was waning, and once the rodeo passed through next weekend, things would quiet down again. Marietta was a glittering little jewel in the fall, when it was quiet and pretty, before the hard snows started.

And this year Sydney would be here too.

They were packed tonight. Folks were already in town for the rodeo, even though official rodeo events didn't begin until a week from now. Jackson liked that rodeo and football drew the same kinds of crowds, in a lot of ways. There were the hardcore passionate fans and the inevitable groupies, but mostly, both events drew in families who might not be able to talk about anything else, but could sit around and talk about the things they saw. They could root for the same winners, despair at the losses, and marvel at the bravery of some of the athletes, human and animal alike.

And rodeos were so much more than that. They fostered community and celebrated the kind of work that went on in and around places like this. The cattle, the livestock. The young kids in 4-H programs and the older ones heading off to agricultural programs at college, so they could come home again and give back to the land that in some cases, generations upon generations of their family had already worked.

Sometimes he imagined having his own kids to share this place with. These silent, watchful mountains. The aspen trees. The river that cut through the town, skateable some winters and a great swim in summer. The simple charms of Main Street.

And he couldn't deny that his own kin were another draw to this place. They were what had brought him here. They were what had kept him here.

Tonight Jasper had taken one of the best tables, sprawling back in his chair and looking entertained by the fact that his wife, the mayor, didn't stay more than a moment or two in her seat before jumping up again, to go talk to this table or that table. Leaving her dinner colder and uneaten every time.

"Do you think she really needs to have all those conversations?" Jackson asked his older brother when he stopped by the table on one of his rounds. "Or does she just want to leave you playing nanny?"

Jasper grinned, looking around the table at the little monsters he called his own. All three of them. The baby, a little girl with her hair in braids and her daddy's cool gaze, was all of three. The two boys—devilish five-year-old Jake and serious, rule-following Jared—were having a currently quiet but soon-to-be loud battle of wills that their father was pretending to ignore.

Three-year-old Jillian had no such qualms. "They're fighting," she told both her daddy and her uncle with wide eyes and angelic voice.

When the truth was, she only looked like an angel.

The truth about little Jillian was that she was a Flint through and through.

"No one likes a tattletale, sweet pea," Jasper drawled, the Texas in his voice mellowed after all these years in Montana, but never gone. He looked up at Jackson. "And a man can't be a nanny to his own children, Jackson. Not any man worth a damn." He looked around the brewery, taking in the happy tables and the band setting up for its second set. "Nice to see the place is kicking."

"It's doing all right," Jackson agreed.

He knew his brother wasn't referring to the brewery itself. The Flint brothers were good at many things, individually and together, but chief among them was making money. The twins had done that, and well. And Jonah had been slower to come to the conclusion his twin had, namely that the kind of money they made only had a purpose if it made the lives they touched a whole lot better than the lives they'd lived so far.

Jackson had reached that conclusion all on his own, thanks in large part to the steady influence of his grandparents, who were the reason he had stayed grounded through the rush of his football days. But he liked the fact that what his brother was really complimenting him on tonight wasn't how much money the brewery would be making tonight, but rather, the fact that FlintWorks had become and remained the kind of gathering place in Marietta Jasper had wanted it to be.

Like a perfect little version of the kind of town Mayor Chelsea—or Mayor Triple-C, as Jasper liked to call her—worked so hard to make it.

Jackson was glad he could be a part of it.

He ruffled his niece's hair a little, just to get her to make a face at him. And then, when he turned around to head back to the kitchen, he stopped dead.

Because finally, *finally*, Sydney was showing her pretty face.

She came in with Emmy Mathis and Griffin Hyatt and the usual band of disreputable-looking tattooed and bearded folks who were, in Jackson's experience, about as true blue a collection of people there was. And she appeared completely unaware that his name was on the door she walked through with a group of people who weren't him.

In point of fact, she seemed to be going out of her way to

act as if she didn't even know he was here.

But Jackson had played this game, with her, more times than he could count.

He knew perfectly well that Sydney was aware of his every breath, the way he was of hers, as surely as if they were tangled up together in his bed.

So once again he ignored every clamoring urge inside him, every taut and winding need, and he didn't go to her. He busied himself behind the bar, and he waited.

And waited.

And tonight he got to watch Sydney playing her games, not *for* him, but *at* him.

More clues for him to ponder, though it was good to remind himself that the goal here was not another long, cold winter of what-ifs. Not this time.

He couldn't say he enjoyed the experience of watching her thing, though she sure did give it her all. He didn't think he'd ever seen her laugh so much. Or with more of her body. She'd even put a little effort into her appearance that he had to think was for his benefit, even though she was doing her level best to pretend otherwise.

But who was he to fail to appreciate what a tank top like that did for her shoulders? Who was he to ask himself what a racerback bra really was, or remind himself that he had developed a particular interest in the one he'd bet she was wearing right now.

It was black. And surprisingly frilly. All lace and longing, to his recollection.

He doubted that was a coincidence either.

But when some of the girls in the group took to the floor to do a little two-stepping with the assorted cowboys and ranch hands Jackson ordinarily counted as friends, he found himself more relieved than he should have been when Sydney excused herself. He watched as she slipped away, down the side corridor that led to the bathrooms, but instead of going in, she kept on going. Straight to the end of the hall and out into the night.

He didn't mean to follow her. But he was only made of flesh and blood, wants and wonder, and somehow it felt like fate when he got out back to find her standing there, her head tilted back to take in the night air.

"You're missing all the dancing," he drawled at her. "Just think how much fun you could have out there, proving beyond any reasonable doubt that you haven't given me a second thought."

She took her time turning back to face him.

"I don't even know who you are," she said. Much too quietly.

He was in the doorway, then he was right there in front of her, and he didn't remember moving.

But he couldn't regret it, either.

"If you pretended that I was someone else, some stranger, would you go on a date with me?" he asked, but he wasn't acting like any kind of stranger. He was acting like he was hers.

He moved in closer, close enough to get his hands on her, but he didn't.

Even though he could smell her scent, something tart and something sweet. Even though he could smell the shampoo she used in her hair. Even though he knew that if he put his mouth to the side of her neck, she would taste like fire.

"I keep telling you," she whispered. "I don't date."

And then Sydney was the one who went up on her toes, pressing her body into his. She wound her arms around his neck, slowly enough that he figured she was making the point that he could have pulled away.

He could have insisted that she go on that date with him first.

He could have, but he didn't.

Because her eyes were full of secrets but he could see the heat there, too.

He could see the whole world.

And maybe she could, too, because she made the soft little noise like something hurt, and then she pressed her lips to his.

It would be so easy to let that fire that always danced between them take them over, take them both away.

It would be the easiest thing in the world to reach down and get his hands on her butt in that way they both liked. To haul her up against him, let her wrap those legs of hers around him, and let it get out of hand the way it always did.

But Jackson wanted more, so he had to show her that there was more.

More restraint, more patience.

They had a lot of the other *mores* covered.

He kissed her, and he loved it when she kissed him too, but he controlled it. He wouldn't let her take it nuclear. He wouldn't let her make them both dizzy and intoxicated.

He kissed her thoroughly, dancing in and around that fire, but never immolating the two of them. Never letting it burn that high.

And it wasn't that it didn't kill him to keep the training wheels on, but he knew that he needed to prove this point here and now or he never would. He wanted too much. He wanted *her* too much.

*The journey, not the destination,* he kept telling himself. *To make the real destination count.*

Until, eventually, she was the one who pulled away, her breath coming fast and ragged there between them.

"You're just making it worse," she muttered, sounding aggrieved and needy and more than a little wild.

He reached down and tapped on her chin, lifting her face so he could look down at her. Because he knew that she liked to pretend that the only information they could share was what was said or not said. What story she told, or withheld.

But he knew better.

He knew that there was this. This thing that had been between them from the start.

And when they looked at each other like this, it took them over. It was a gleaming kind of wonder, and it filled every bit of space between them until there was nothing left but truth.

A truth he knew all too well, no matter what demands his body kept trying to make.

"If you want to kiss me, you're going to have to date me," he told her, and he didn't sound any less wild or needy. And only slightly less aggrieved. "I'm pretty sure I made that clear."

"I'm so sorry that I impugned your virtue," she said, grandly enough that he grinned. "And I'm here, aren't I? In a brewery where people do things. Date things. They're in there doing them right now."

"You want this to be a date? Then it has to be an actual date." She scowled at him, and his grin widened, but she didn't look away. That felt like progress. "You said you were rusty on this stuff, so let me be clear. A date is not you at a table full of other people, pretending you don't see me."

"I saw you." He watched the color rise in her cheeks. "I just didn't attach any meaning to that sighting."

"Sure you didn't." His hands were still on her, so Jackson told himself it was a test. One he could pass, and not just because he was good at taking tests. But because he wanted to be good at this, too. He wanted to be good at *her*. At *them*. So he didn't let go. He kept his hands where they were, letting his thumbs trace a little pattern on her bare shoulders.

And the way she shivered felt a whole lot like a reward. "A date isn't separating yourself from the pack and hoping someone comes after you."

"I'm not a wounded gazelle on the savanna, Jackson." Her clever gaze met his, and she lifted a brow. "And if I was, you do realize that makes you the predator in this scenario, right?"

He refused to let her derail all this virtue he was expending. "A date involves a leisure activity, Sydney. One you generally have with the person you're on a date with. Having a burger with your friends, and then kissing me out back in the dark? That doesn't count."

She shrugged. "Felt like it counted to me."

"There is usually something to eat or drink," he continued with exaggerated patience. "Like I'm pretty sure I mentioned, there's the conversation. That's the getting-to-know-you part. They all go together. And if they go together well, guess what? Then there's kissing."

She rocked back on her heels and crossed her arms, but she didn't step back in a way that would signal he ought to drop his hands. So he didn't.

Instead, she looked up at him. And he wasn't sure he'd ever seen this particular expression on her face. She looked... out of sorts.

This was not the Sydney who could smile at him sexily from beneath her bangs, sometimes from across a room, and rearrange the cells in his body. This was not the Sydney who watched him sleepily as he cooked her food and sometimes fed it to her, too. This was not even the Sydney he'd dropped off at the airport in Bozeman a time or two, her gaze blank and her smile nothing but polite.

If he had to guess—and he wouldn't, not out loud, not where his speculation would spook her—Jackson might be tempted to think that this was the real Sydney.

Sydney without a mask.

And wasn't she a sight for sore eyes. Pretty enough to make his chest ache.

"Fine. I can throw down with the weird, personal information if that's the new rule, though you might regret it." She managed to sound put upon and irritated, but she didn't stop. "As far as I've ever been aware, everyone in Marietta knows the story of my grandparents. Grandpa with his famous wandering eye. Grandma, a shroud of doom and gloom, who gives storms a run for their money."

"Elly and Richard," Jackson said at once, with a nod. "I haven't spent any time with the two of them, but I've heard stories like anyone else. The Greys have a reputation around here."

"My grandma has always maintained that we're all cursed," Sydney told him, and her chin tilted up like she was throwing down some kind of dare. "That it's in our blood, thanks to Grandpa. She got married at eighteen and the way she tells it, every day since has been nothing but enough torture to put an early Christian martyr to shame. Still, she took it personally when three of her four children couldn't stay married. And then there's my mom, who only seems to have settled down in the last five years. Somehow, she's never managed to put together that the way she and Grandpa hate each other—or, really, the way she hates him but stays with him—might have had an effect on her children. And all of us cousins, too, because we were raised by the damaged people she raised."

Then she stared at him. Like she expected him to back away, hands raised, then disappear forever.

"We all have family wounds, Sydney," Jackson drawled instead. "It's just a question of how we deal with them as we go along. Are they scars, white and small and more art than injury? Or are they still bleeding?"

"It's funny you should say that." And this was a Sydney he'd never seen before, he realized then, as she shifted there before him. The one who was usually hidden away somewhere in Washington DC, doing secret things and, he'd bet anything, vibrating with excitement of one sort or another, just like this. "My grandparents' 70th anniversary is next weekend. The Copper Mountain Rodeo weekend."

She shrugged a little, he wasn't sure if that was a defensive gesture, or more an invitation to go along with her. He found both possibilities endearing.

"I can just… *feel* the threads knit themselves together. That always happens when I'm on the right track. I knew that there was something there. My grandparents and the rodeo, at some point over the past seventy years. So I did what I do best." Something flared in her gaze as she looks at him. "Research, before your mind goes into the gutter."

"I think it's your mind that's in the gutter, darlin'."

She huffed out a little laugh at that. "Anyway, I found something. A picture that tells… way more than a thousand words, but none of them words that my grandmother would ever say. Or want me to say, I'm pretty sure."

Sydney stepped back then. Jackson let his hands drop, because it was that or make it much too clear how little he ever wanted to lose contact with her. But in the next moment, he realized that she was focused on something else.

Because she was scowling, but not at him. "Meanwhile, I've been here for days. Officially more days than I've spent in Marietta in years. And there are certain realities that I can't escape. It's still summer, more or less, and Big Sky is… what? A couple of hours away? That's with clear roads, no ice, no snow. My grandparents won't accept help. Their mobility is significantly less than it used to be. My uncle Ryan and aunt Gracie want to move them back to Marietta. That's where they live. That's where Uncle Jason and Luce are too. This is where we have the high concentration of family around here—which, I'm pretty sure, is one reason they moved away in the first place—and it makes perfect sense for them to be where people can check on them. But of course they won't hear of it. They don't even want to have the conversation."

Jackson knew perfectly well that she'd never let him see her like this before. This... agitated and consumed with something that wasn't how they were going to get naked. It wasn't as if she was throwing a fit here. It was just that this was real. And real was something she only let happen if it was physical.

His heart skipped a beat, because she was doing it. She was doing the thing she'd been so sure she couldn't.

"When my mama was dying there came a time when she needed to go to hospice," he said. And he said it quietly, though it wasn't a secret. He was sure he'd told her before, because it wasn't something he hid. Or even hid from. But he knew, the same as she did, it was different now. Out here in the dark tonight, where she was showing him parts of her she never had before. "She didn't want to do it. And of course, we didn't want her to do it. But she had to make the call. And I think, looking back, that she waited longer than she should have because she knew what it meant once that call was made."

Sydney shook her head, as if this was all too much. His past, her present. "You think it's okay if you live far away. If you come home when it matters. And you string the visits together in your memory, like some kind of necklace, where everything is the same polished, pretty little stone. But life is a lot more complicated than that. It never occurred to me that choosing to stay away is the same thing as hiding."

"Not the same thing," Jackson argued. "Life is complicated. I don't think I need to tell you that. There's not one thing I've ever heard about Elly and Richard Grey that leads me to think they'd take kindly to it if all of the grandchildren were hanging around like it was already a wake."

She actually laughed at that, and it felt like a victory. A triumph above and beyond all others.

"They would hate that. Vocally and at great length."

"It is easier with small children, or so I'm told," Jackson said then, though her laughter was in him now, like something bright and shiny and his. "You're supposed to keep them alive. When it comes to the end of a life, it's the opposite. I don't think any of us are built for that. So we all stumble around, doing it the best we can and second-guessing it after."

She looked at him for a long moment then. And he could *feel* it. It was raw and it was too big. And it sat there between them, maybe not as filled with wonder, but far more fascinating for all the layers now. Dangerous, he thought she'd call it, though he'd call it something else.

Intimate, maybe.

He expected her to do something to soften it. To make it less of an ache. Or less revealing, somehow.

But she didn't. "My grandmother has dined out on the fact that she doesn't believe in love, only vows made and kept, for the whole of her life. However much of a hard-ass you think an old woman can be, multiply that by infinity, and that's Grandma. She's not cozy. She's never been cuddly.

The only thing I can say she's been, with absolute certainty, is disgusted with my grandfather. From day one."

She reached back and pulled her phone out of her pocket. Then she swiped until she could turn it around to present him with a picture on the screen.

It was grainy, a snapshot of a black-and-white photo in an old newspaper. Once that clicked, the setting did, too. If he wasn't mistaken, the couple in the picture, young and bright, were dancing on Main Street like the whole town would be next week after the barbecue. Looking like there was nothing else in the whole world but the two of them.

"Are these your grandparents?"

Sydney nodded, slowly. "I have proof that for at least one moment in time, my grandparents were crazy in love. With each other. And yet if I share this with them, on the anniversary of their marriage seventy years on, my grandmother will never forgive me. Because I can guarantee you, Jackson, that Elly Grey wants nothing more than to die as mad and as bitter as she's been for every moment of those seventy years, save this one."

She looked down at the phone in her hand, then tucked it away in her back pocket again.

"Does this feel like a date?" she asked then. "Is this the kind of getting-to-know-you conversation you were hoping for?"

He wanted to touch her, but he didn't dare. Not then. Not with that rawness between them, and the intensity of the things she was saying crackling all around them.

And he could see that she thought she'd proved something here. That she'd showed him how foolish he was to think she was the kind of woman who would ever *date*. That there was a reason everything between them was late-night bars and no morning afters.

But she was wrong.

"It's not a terrible thing to be known," he told her instead, because she needed to hear it. "To let other people know you. I promise."

As he watched, her eyes got too bright, with an emotion he couldn't name. And knew she wouldn't.

"You can't promise that, Jackson. You *can't*." Her voice was low, then. Scratchy. Not hers at all—or maybe, he corrected himself, more her than she'd ever showed him before. "The people who've known me, it turns out, thought it was pretty terrible. And they proved it, too."

"Then they didn't know you at all," he told her with absolute, bedrock certainty, his gaze fixed to hers like he could make her see what he did. "It was themselves they were having trouble getting a handle on. But there's not one single thing I could ever know about you that I would ever call terrible, Sydney."

And right there, he thought emotion was going to get the better of her. This wild intensity, snapping all around them on a clear end-of-summer evening, was going to make her run away from him the way she always did, and he didn't want that. Not now.

"You don't have to believe me," he told her, and he made himself smile. To take the temperature down, just a little. Just enough. "I welcome the opportunity to prove it to you. One date at a time."

# Chapter Six

THE NEXT DAY, Sydney caught a ride to Big Sky with Luce, who had been dispatched to talk sense into Elly and Richard.

"No sense has ever been spoken to the pair of them," Luce said as they headed out of Marietta. "And believe me, better women than I have tried. My mother is *nice*. I am… me."

"I'm going to appeal to the good memories they have," Sydney announced to Luce's windshield. "To see if maybe they want to make a few more good memories before they're not capable of it anymore."

"Yeah," Luce said, rolling her eyes. "That sounds like them. That'll work for sure."

The pretty-much-daily breakfasts at her aunt and uncle's had been a lot like that these past few days. Ryan and Gracie had convened all the family members in town for a little summit meeting, since Sydney's presence meant another branch of the family was represented. That meant even Uncle Jason made an appearance, always acting like he was vying for the Elly Grey award for most surliness possible in an enclosed space.

Something he did not find funny when Sydney said it out loud.

"I know you think you can make Mom and Dad do something they don't want to do," Jason had said to Ryan. In various ways. Repeatedly. Today he'd sounded even grimmer than usual. "And I admire your optimism. I really do. But you've never been realistic where that was concerned."

"Here's what's realistic," Gracie had chimed in before Ryan could answer—hotly, if the look on his face was anything to go by. "One of them is going to fall. How they've made it through this many winters without anything catastrophic happening already, I will never know. What happens then? Or worse, if both of them fall? The trouble is, all the way out there, there's no way we'll know about it in time. And even if we did, depending on the weather, we couldn't get to them."

"Have you thought about that?" Ryan had demanded, glaring around the table, but mostly at Jason, when Ryan was usually the most relaxed of the uncles. "Not even about falling down. About what will happen when, not if, one of them goes?"

Jason had stared back at him. "I think about that all the time. If it was Dad alone, we'd get him over here to Marietta, no problem. He'd be just as happy to live in the bar as anywhere else. Your guest room, Ryan." He'd looked over at Luce. "Probably not yours." He'd taken his time looking back at his brother. "But Mom? I think she'll stay out in that house to the bitter end, because you might not remember this, but she built it in the first place to isolate Dad. I don't see her giving that up, even if what she's isolating is herself."

Gracie and Ryan had looked at each other for a moment, giving Sydney the distinct impression that they hadn't believed for even one moment that anyone had thought about the state of Elly and Richard but them. It seemed to take them a moment to recalibrate.

Sydney had taken that as her cue to smile. "Then it seems like the only possible way to get them to leave that house is if they do it together. Maybe there's a way we can convince them that they should."

That was how she and Luce had been volunteered—or, rather, volun-*told*—for today's outreach program. As Gracie had called it.

"It's an appeal to their better natures, that's all," she'd said.

Cue a whole lot of rolled eyes and snorts from the peanut gallery.

But it was a beautiful day today, and there wasn't much better than Montana on a wild blue September morning. They drove up through funky Livingston at the top of Paradise Valley, stopping only to grab coffee and something sweet at their favorite little bakery. Then they followed the interstate for a little while before heading south again and following the Gallatin River all the way into the valley until they reached Big Sky. They both sang along to the songs on the radio, and sometimes at each other, and for a while there, speeding down remote mountain roads with the Rockies pressing in all around them like more members of their extended family, it could have been any year at all.

Or all the years Sydney had come here or missed coming here, all wrapped up into two sunny, blue hours.

When they wound their way up the side of the mountain to the house that legend really did claim that Elly Grey had built out of spite, Sydney wasn't sure if her heart felt better than it had. Or if she was just feeling it a whole lot more than before.

And she could have pretended that she hadn't spent most of the drive singing her face off and thinking too much about Jackson, but that would have been a lie.

She thought about kissing him. She thought about telling him things she normally treated like state secrets. She thought about the way he'd looked at her…

God, did she get lost in the way he looked at her.

But today was about her grandparents, not… whatever Jackson was. She and Luce climbed out of the car, stretched in the mountain air that was cool enough, up this high, to suggest that Montana's fall was already settling in. They let themselves in the front door that was never locked, something that made Sydney shudder from the inside out, calling out as they went.

"Don't know why I bother," Luce muttered. "They think

they can hear, but they can't."

They found their grandparents sitting in the kitchen, where the sun streamed in and brought the aspens in with it. Grandpa was sitting at the old, scarred wood table, cleaning tools with his gnarled, arthritic hands. Elly stood at the counter, assembling a meal. Lunch, Sydney knew, because her grandparents liked their meals at certain, set times.

Grandpa looked up and made a low noise of approval, smiling at the sight of two of his granddaughters. As they both went to kiss him hello, Elly only looked at them coolly. She straightened as if shouldering a burden, then set about making another sandwich. She cut it in half, then spooned out bowls of the soup she had bubbling on the stove, carrying it to the table and setting it before Luce, then Sydney. Then Grandpa.

"I wish you lived closer," Luce said with a smile that made her look like a serial killer. "I would kill for some of this soup every day in winter, Grandma."

"I'll thank you not to patronize me, Lucille Marie," Elly snapped back.

Luce rolled her eyes—no doubt at her full name—and then she and Grandpa started talking about her boys, and the sports Grandpa thought they should involve themselves in so as to carouse a bit less.

"As the reigning expert," Grandma murmured serenely. To her soup.

Sydney smiled at her grandmother, the woman everyone

said Sydney resembled more than anyone else in the family. She was the one who'd gotten the red hair Grandma had sported in her youth. They were even shaped the same, though Grandma tended toward elegance and Sydney considered herself slight and usually too skinny.

Today, looking at Grandma, like a mirror into her own future, made her feel almost… overwhelmed. Ragged inside, like she might just… burst into tears.

That was much too weird, and she really didn't want to dig into it, so she pulled out her phone, found the picture, and slid it on the tabletop between them. "I was looking around in the library archives these past few days. They have a lot of old newspapers."

"I've always thought that the primary use of old newspapers was to burn things," Grandma said starchily, because Uncle Jason's sullenness and general bad mood didn't come from thin air. "They don't even have to be that old, to my mind."

Sydney didn't have to catch Luce's sideways look to feel it burn the side of her face. She tapped at the screen of her phone instead. "I'm glad they didn't burn all of them. Or I never would've found this picture of you and Grandpa."

Her grandmother stared down at the phone as if it was a poisonous snake that Sydney had taken upon herself to throw into the center of the table. On her other side, Grandpa reached out and pulled the phone closer to him, peered at it, then made a soft sort of exclamation.

"Well, look at that," he said, sounding warmed straight through, as pleased as pie. "I remember it like it was yesterday. You and me, Elly. Dancing the night away on Main Street in Marietta, with the rodeo in town and the whole world our oyster."

"I'm sure I don't remember anything of the kind."

But if Grandpa heard the stiffness in his wife's voice, he ignored it. He grinned at the picture, then at his granddaughters—who were doing their best not to stare at each other in amazement. "Look at your grandmother, girls. As pretty as a picture. You can hardly recognize her now, but I remember."

Luce laughed as if that was funny, but Sydney had been looking at the picture a lot longer than her cousin. And it was true. Elly was unrecognizable, almost, for a lot of reasons.

In the picture, she looked *happy*. She had her head thrown back and it felt as if you just listened hard, you might hear her laughter in the distance. Maybe even as tinkling and pretty as Melody's was always said to be. And everyone was beautiful when they were young, or so it seemed to Sydney who spent a lot of time looking at archival footage, but the fact was that Elly had been more than simply flushed with youth and the attention of a handsome man. She was genuinely pretty. Recognizably pretty.

The more Sydney looked at the picture and then at Grandma, the more she realized that Melody looked just like her mother. Beautiful, impossible Melody, who had grown up with the bitter ruins of the pretty girl in this picture.

And maybe it wasn't such a surprise, then, that she had caused a bit of wreckage herself. Sydney wasn't sure she liked feeling a reluctant little pang of sympathy for her mother. It made Melody less of a figure in her life and more… human. Real.

Her throat was dry and the hot soup didn't help as much as she thought it should.

"That picture is a lie," Elly pronounced, after staring down at it in clear condemnation for some while. "I have no idea why you would bring it here like this."

As if it was something dirty and shameful. Or possibly poisonous.

"Happy anniversary?" Luce ventured dryly. "You have been married for seventy years, Grandma. Sometimes—and believe me, I know this is a stretch—people like to celebrate that kind of thing."

"There's nothing to celebrate." Grandma pushed back from the table, making the chair screech along the floor. "I was a young fool when I got married. That's all there is to it. And believe me, fools get taken advantage of, and so I was."

"Now, Elly," Grandpa began, the way he always did.

But Grandma looked like she was getting on one of her rolls. Her eyes were flashing. She drew herself up to her full height, which, now that she was very old, was not very high at all. And while her hair was no longer red at all, Sydney was sure she could see the memory of it, like a ghost.

A ghost that looked like her. And her mother.

"There's only one constant in this life, and that's that it carries on until it's done," Elly was saying. "That's what marriage is. That's what life is. The only thing you have is the knowledge that you were either a good person, who kept her vows and her promises." She glared at Grandpa. "Or you were not."

He waved a hand at her as if to brush that away, and looked back to his tools. He looked unbothered, but then, he always did. Maybe that was how they'd made it seventy years.

"That's pretty grim, Grandma," Luce said after the words had time to settle in. "Even for you."

Sydney was shaking her head, maybe a little more agitated than she wanted to admit. And maybe she wouldn't have admitted it. She was starting to realize that not admitting things was something she was pretty frighteningly good at.

But all of a sudden, she was just… talking. Right to her grandmother. "I don't understand," she heard herself say. "Seventy years, Grandma. *Seventy whole years* when you're miserable. What's the point? Suffering is supposed to end, isn't it?"

She should never have asked that. Because all it did was give her grandmother an opportunity to go off on one of her favorite rants. It covered the lot of women and the inconstancy of men, and how the measure of a life wasn't happiness—whatever that was, and she always let out a huff of amazement that people these days put such stock in *happiness*, by God—but in demonstrating hard work and sacrifice, no matter what.

It took them an hour to get out of there.

"So much for talking about moving back to Marietta," Luce muttered as they slunk back out toward the car.

"It's almost like she goes out of her way to make sure that's not a topic that can ever be discussed," Sydney muttered back.

They went outside, gulping in the fresh, clean mountain air. The view from this house was spectacular, no matter the season, and today was no different. They stood there for a while, gazing out at the mountains, the valley below with the wild river cutting its way through the earth, and the gold and green and high blue splendor of Montana rolling out in every direction.

And when they turned to climb into Luce's car, Grandpa had come out from the side of the house to meet them. He was shuffling along, not as spry as he was in Sydney's memories, but not as rickety as most men his age, either.

"Don't mind your grandmother," he said gruffly as he pulled close, still smelling of leather. Still wearing a button-down shirt and a cowboy hat, the way he had been every time she'd laid eyes on him out of doors in as long as she could remember. "She might be a masochist, but I'm not."

"Aren't you?" Luce asked at once, because of course she

would. And did. "Are you sure you know what the word means, Grandpa?"

He looked down at the ground for a moment, as if debating what to say. Or maybe how to say it. But when he looked up again, Sydney was sure that he was looking straight at her.

"Your grandmother is a hard woman," he said, but it wasn't a complaint. It didn't even sound like a criticism "There's no denying that. And pretty as she was at eighteen, it was just a pretty cover for the fact she was hard then, too. Like granite."

They all stood there with that for a moment. Up above, a crow made itself known. Another one answered.

"Well," Luce said, drawing the word out. "I guess that's a good thing?"

Their grandfather laughed. "I'm a native Montanan. Hard has never worried me much. I have myself a hard head, so I don't mind a few knocks as I go."

"Romantic," Luce said. "Truly."

"A lifetime of hard is nothing," Grandpa said, his mouth curving, like he knew things they didn't. A whole lot of things. Things Sydney wasn't sure she wanted to think about in the context of her *grandparents*. And he wasn't done. "Not next to a few moments, scattered here and there, of sweet. Sweeter than you can possibly imagine." He looked out toward the view, then back at them, and Sydney found she couldn't see the old man he was now. Because there on his face was that young man in the picture, dancing and laughing, forever. When he caught them looking, he smiled. "Don't let anyone tell you different."

And she and Luce were on the interstate again before Luce turned down the music, and said, in tones of awe, "I think that Grandpa and Grandma might actually be..."

But she couldn't finish.

"I know," Sydney said in the same sort of voice. "It's some messed up, endlessly complicated, seventy years of a love story that as far as I can tell? That makes sense only to them?"

Her cousin laughed at that, turning up the music once again. "Good for them, then." She shot Sydney a look as she drove faster than necessary toward Paradise Valley. "Who else should have to make sense of it but the people involved?"

And that was what sat with Sydney when Luce dropped her off at the Graff some time later.

She made her way up to her beautiful hotel room and sat there, alone, looking at pictures of long dead people staring back at her from daguerreotypes on the walls. Luce's words wound their way into her as she showered, then got dressed.

Because maybe she'd spent far too much time focused on wreckage and how to avoid it, when that had never been the point. Maybe the point was what had always been around it. The bright days. The happy times.

Maybe she'd inherited a little too much of her grandma's

scowl and not enough of her mother's shine.

Because despite the whole life she'd made out of analyzing and disseminating information, maybe, just maybe, none of the things that mattered were supposed to be understood. Seventy years of a relationship that defied description. Her mother finally settling down. Uncle Jason cozy as he could be with his darkness, and not afraid to let everyone see it.

Maybe it wasn't about understanding any of that. Maybe what mattered was the way she'd felt when she'd seen that picture. Because it was tender, and raw, and revealing, and she was sure she looked at Jackson the same way.

So she found her way out onto Main Street and walked over to the train depot, but didn't go up to the studio set above it. She kept on going, walking into FlintWorks. It had only just opened for the evening and was still relatively quiet. His bar staff was there. The tables were filled with a decent selection of people, and she found she recognized a lot of them. Like she was already halfway to a local, the way she'd always secretly felt she was. Or ought to have been, no matter where she actually lived.

But she really only had eyes for Jackson.

He looked up at her, saw that she was looking right at him, and smiled.

"Jackson Flint," she said, fully aware that she was speaking loudly enough that everyone in FlintWorks could hear her. Because that had to be the next best thing to a picture. And this way, her whole family would be sure to know within minutes. "Would you like to go on a date with me?"

And for the longest, most terrifying moment, everything was still. Everything except her racing heart and spinning head, and that voice inside of her that reminded her that she hadn't prepared herself—at all—for the very real possibility that he might say no.

She had no idea what she would do.

But a grin broke over his face. And there was pure fire in his eyes. "Sydney Campbell," he replied, with a little more Texas in his drawl than usual. "I thought you'd never ask."

There was some applause at that. Some actual hooting and hollering, that she saw came from the back, where one of his twin older brothers stood. Jasper, from the context clues. That being the mayor there with him.

The applause only got louder when Jackson vaulted over the bar, making no secret of his haste to get to her.

"How's right now?" he asked, and Sydney had a sudden memory, then, of one of her college roommates talking with great disdain about how unattractive *enthusiasm* was in a man.

Sydney wasn't sure she'd ever seen anything hotter.

She smiled up at him. "Only if you're not busy."

"Not at all, darlin'," he drawled, to more applause and a few choice words from his brother, delivered with a laugh and the mayor's blessing.

Sydney didn't date, but this was Jackson. And she kept telling herself, as the panic swelled up inside her, that she didn't have to *understand* this. She only had to do it, because it felt like she might actually, literally die if she didn't.

He took her hand and led her back outside. And she didn't have to understand anything except how nice it was to walk with him through town. Hiding nothing. Simply enjoying him, there beside her, which was right where she wanted him. There was no pretending she didn't know him, no waiting for him to show up.

She had gone to him and she had asked him to go out with her, and there was a remarkable power in that, because here they were.

And maybe that was why it seemed like everything fell into place around them.

They found a table in the Italian place, tucked away in a dark corner, where she got lost in him. If there were other people in the restaurant, she never knew it.

He told her stories of growing up in Texas. Of his football career, which was funny and poignant, exciting and a little bit sad.

"Don't you wish they were still doing it?" she asked.

"Sure," he said, as if nostalgia was normal. Easy. He reached across the table to pick up her hand and toyed with her fingers, which she told herself sternly she shouldn't allow—but she couldn't remember why not. "But if I was still doing that, I wouldn't be doing this. And the thing about football is that, like a lot of things, you can do it well only for a very short period of time. No matter how good you are. Most guys can't imagine what their life will look like on the other side of that, so they hold on as long as they can. But I'm not most guys."

"No," Sydney said quietly. "I don't think you are."

And then, in the spirit of all this great communication, and because she forgot to warn herself against it, she found herself telling him stories about her own childhood. Not just the lovely summers here in Montana, but the strange nomadic existence she and Devyn had been towed along in. The new schools. The inevitable moment when their new classmates realized that the loony woman waiting for them every now and again was, in fact, their mother. But she only averaged a few appearances at things like teacher meetings or school pickups, and that only made it more noticeable when her attention got caught somewhere else.

Which it always did.

She told him about that stepbrother they'd had, Vaughn Taylor, during another period of almost normal—and that he'd grown up to marry Devyn. She told him about that infamous 50th birthday party in Jackson Hole and how she'd done her level best not to attend, but in the end, couldn't leave her sister to suffer through the madness on her own.

"And I'm glad you didn't," he said. "Because I would never have heard any of these stories."

And much later, when they looked up to find—with some astonishment—that the restaurant was closing all around them, they walked out into the streets again. And this time, their fingers seem to tangle together of their own accord.

They walked quietly for a time, side by side. And once again, Sydney felt it in her heart. Like a good song played loud. Like the sort of nostalgia that didn't hurt. Like that picture of her grandparents dancing, light and free, like other people.

"What turned you around on the dating thing?" he asked as they walked.

She felt something shivering her, like foreboding. Or something else. Maybe hope, though she would have said she didn't believe in it.

Sydney stopped, there in front of a pretty little chocolate shop.

"The thing is, Jackson," she found herself whispering, as if the stars up high were listening. "I don't want seventy years of much too hard with only a few moments of sweet. That sounds like terrible math."

He looked at her the way he sometimes did, as if he was bemused. As if he couldn't quite make sense of her, but he liked it anyway. He reached over and traced the line of her face, from temple to chin. And there was a light in his eyes, in the way he looked at her.

And if this wasn't hope, she wasn't sure she'd ever felt it.

Sydney had never felt so much like begging before in her life. And she couldn't have said for what.

But she also knew that this man actually did know her.

He'd insisted on it. And because he did, she didn't have to hide the fact that she was emotional and wavering. He had called this a date and that meant he might take her to bed.

God, she hoped he would.

Because surely what she needed more than anything right now was the oblivion that only he could bring.

*Right,* came that annoying voice in her head. *Oblivion. That's why it's so raw you have to run out before dawn, every time.*

"Walk with me," Jackson said softly.

And this time, he didn't stop at the door to the Graff. He walked her inside, then into the ancient elevator that rattled so much as it rose that it was tempting to think it might trap them here. Where, oh well, they'd have nothing to do but hope they lived.

And celebrate maybe not living as best they could.

She was still daydreaming about exactly how that celebration would go when they stopped in front of her door.

"Jackson…" she began.

"This was a great date," he told her, and the heat and approval in his voice made her feel… silly. "My best yet, I don't mind telling you."

Then he pulled her close, tipped her so her back was against her own door, and took her mouth with his.

It was like catapulting straight off into space.

On the back of a rocket.

Jackson kissed her and he kissed her, leaning in and getting his hands around her face so he could hold her where he wanted her. Then he pressed the length of that beautiful body of his against hers, crowding her against the door in the most wonderful way imaginable.

He wasn't pacing her the way he had done the last time. He wasn't holding back.

But all the same, he pulled away.

Sydney didn't know if she was devastated or delighted. Because it seemed like he was keeping his promise, and she hated that.

She was sure she hated it.

He smiled, though she thought it hurt him. "I really don't want to go, darlin'." But he shook his head when she moved toward him. "Which is why I will."

She lifted her hand to her face, because she wanted to… Do something about her eyes, maybe. Or possibly punch him. But she realized when she could see her own hand in front of her that it was shaking. Trembling. Just like her knees, now that she was taking stock.

She tried to scowl at him. "I don't want all this nobility, you know."

Jackson leaned in close. He pressed a kiss to her temple, her cheek.

And when he spoke, it was a rumble she could feel deep inside her and all over her. "But Sydney, baby, you need it. That's the point."

Then, once again, she watched him walk away from her.

But this time, to her great surprise, she was smiling while she watched him go.

# Chapter Seven

HAVING NEVER DATED anyone before, Sydney certainly didn't know what to expect.

But dating Jackson wasn't anything like what she'd feared.

It was a wild blue September in Montana, with nights that grew ever colder and an aching, golden sunlight that made the mountains seem to glow as if they, too, couldn't wait for the coming Copper Mountain Rodeo that had all of Marietta buzzing with excitement.

Sydney didn't exactly turn into a die-hard rodeo fan overnight, but she liked the buzz.

It seemed to match what was happening inside her.

Because this sweet life she was trying on for size seemed to fit almost too well, and she thought that ought to terrify her. It was so different from the life she'd built for herself in DC. She spent most mornings checking in with her family, both near and far. Because her cousins had all gotten wind of the movement to get Elly and Richard out of Big Sky and back home to Marietta to live out what time they had left, and most of them had decided that Sydney was the one to discuss their feelings with.

"I want them to do what they feel is right," her cousin Skylar, always the calm voice of reason in the family—despite her shocker of a marriage to a bull rider of uncertain reputation, who seemed to love her wildly and fully.

*Well,* Luce had said at their wedding, *this is not what anyone could have predicted. But that man is* HOT.

This was an indisputable fact. Cody Galen was a whole thing, and Skylar was the only one to tame him.

"They always do what *they* feel is right," Skylar's sister Scottie, a high-powered attorney in San Francisco, chimed in then. "That doesn't mean it's good for them. And I'm sorry to say that sometimes, it's incumbent upon the younger generations to look out for their elders." They'd been on a video call, so Sydney watched as she shrugged, moving documents around in her office. "I'll look into the power of attorney situation."

"I'll call them and make sure they're okay," Skylar replied with a little of that steel that she'd developed in recent years.

Reminding Sydney not only that people *could* change, but that Skylar, who had always seemed gentle and obliging and all the things most of the rest of them were not, was a Grey straight through. And not hiding it any longer.

"Great," Sydney murmured. "Glad I could be here for this chat between you two."

But she laughed when she said it, and her cousins laughed with her.

"Luce is impossible," her cousin Jesse said in a phone call later in that I Am So Powerful And Seattle Trembles Before Me voice of his. She didn't think he was putting it on. Every time he called he sounded like he was standing in the middle of something *critically important*, but had somehow managed to carve out a little space for this phone call. Some people in the family—namely Skylar and Scottie, his younger sisters—found that annoying. But if Sydney was honest, it reminded her of… herself. "If I wanted to hear treatises on why divorcing at ninety is a healthy option they ought to consider, I would ask for them."

"Some people are only capable of seeing the world through their own lens," Sydney said, with great diplomacy.

There was silence on the phone. "Who are you?" Jesse asked. "And what have you done with my robotic cousin Sydney, who as far as I know is actually a computer? Or an android?"

"Listen," Sydney said. "Marietta is a magical kind of place."

Jesse laughed. "That it is."

And they talked for a minute about the usual family undercurrents, above and beyond what was going on with their grandparents. And when she hung up, Sydney sat cross-legged in the middle of her bed in her hotel room, feeling completely unlike herself. Because she was not, in fact, an android, though she was aware that she'd been playing one for years now.

She didn't know precisely when that had happened. When she'd decided that was the better option than… any of the other options. Or maybe she'd just figured that since she spent so much time on and with computers, she might as well emulate them.

But this little foray into acting like a human felt good.

She was thinking about Jesse as she walked outside and climbed into her rented car, so she could drive up to Ryan and Gracie's place for the now routine family gathering that had turned into a daily thing.

Jesse had been the most cursed of the Grey cousins, by some accounts, after the girlfriend he'd brought home for Christmas one year had ended up marrying his father instead. But then he'd taken part in a Valentine's Day charity event in Marietta, had driven back to Seattle with the woman who'd "bought" him at said event, and look at that. He and Michaela made happy ever after look easy.

Sydney pulled into the driveway of Gracie and Ryan's place, and stopped as she got out of the car. This house was in a neighborhood on a hill above town and it was fun to look down at Marietta, sparkling there in all its glory. She let out a deep breath and thought about the fact that when people asked her where she came from, she never mentioned Baltimore, where her father lived. Or any of the places she'd lived with her mother.

She always claimed Marietta as her hometown. She still did.

And the funniest thing about people who lived in cities, to her mind, was how they prided themselves on tolerances of all kinds but couldn't seem to fathom why it was that people would live in places that weren't cities. They talked a lot about *ending up* in towns like Marietta. About lacking the imagination to leave. But it was Sydney's observation that it was the city people who panicked at the notion that they might have to live somewhere without the twenty-four-hour services they liked to know were available, even if they never used them. It was the city people who preferred the excuse of anonymity to act as if they had no social ties to anyone, and could therefore behave as antisocial and rude as they liked—all in the name of being important city people with places to go.

In Marietta, the person you were rude to was likely to be going to the same place that you were, so it was smarter all around to stay polite, if not kind.

Washington DC was an exemplar of that kind of city person, because DC was one hundred percent that kind of city—which was funny, really, because Sydney knew that there wasn't a city around that wasn't filled with people convinced that there was no greater power than whatever power it was they thought they wielded.

And yet, what Sydney knew was that people craved community. People who worked her job, for example, took pride in having no life outside the office. There were always those who actually tried, and was never a surprise when those people—with those impossible ties to expectations outside the work they did—were dragged in opposing directions. Privately, everyone else was proud that they didn't suffer from the same fate.

But they had each other. Sydney wouldn't call on any of her colleagues to save her from a fire or to offer her a helping hand, unless it was work related. But if work was all a person did, that was the community that a person had. That was the community she'd had, for years.

She couldn't regret all the time she'd spent there.

But Marietta was something else.

It sat in her much, much differently, like snow and sunlight.

And it was such an oddly beautiful, surprising gift to come back to a place that she associated with the summers of her childhood. Summers that she'd loved, when she'd loved very few things about growing up in Melody's chaotic orbit and her father's distant house. She was slightly worried that there was a danger in spending too much time in a memory, one that would reveal itself in time even if she couldn't see it now

But that wasn't the experience she was having.

She had to think that Jackson was a huge part of why that was.

Because every night, she and Jackson would have another sort of date. And sometimes he would turn up during the day, insisting that they have coffee.

And it was all so silly, and so sweet. He held her hand. He opened doors for her. And he kissed her—oh, how he kissed her—until her bones felt like they might melt, and her heart hurt, and sometimes he even moved his hands restlessly over her body in a way she found familiar and delightful—

But he never took it any further, because apparently he was made of stone.

The more annoyingly noble he was, the more she scowled at him and complained.

And then, when she was alone, the more that bright little thread of hope inside of her seemed to take root. Until it was tied in knots, bright and gleaming, as if daring her to tug on it.

Or to let it grow.

"Are you coming inside?" her uncle Jason asked then, jolting her out of her memories of last night's meltingly good kiss. He scowled at her as he climbed out of truck. "Or are you in a trance?"

"Just enjoying this beautiful day!" she chirped at him, as cheerfully as possible, for the express purpose of getting his usual black cloud response.

She was still grinning like a fool as she followed him into the house.

"You must be going out of your mind," her sister Devyn said in a different phone call later, because Devyn liked to check in at least once a day. Not only because she thought Sydney was mid-breakdown. But also, probably, because she couldn't believe Sydney was out here doing the family thing.

Repeatedly. Deliberately.

And would likely be continuing to do it for weeks on end. After all, while Devyn was always considered the responsible one in their little branch of the family tree, *she* lived in Nashville.

"Why do you say that?" Sydney asked, not surprised that she sounded a little edgy. The question rubbed her the wrong way, if she was honest. She'd spent most of the day fielding phone calls from various cousins while trying to keep her uncles from getting into an actual brawl. Now she was walking down Main Street, heading for her shift at Grey's.

She felt decidedly sane, as a matter fact. And maybe a little too responsible, thank you, which was not supposed to be her role. Historically.

"This is just so not you," Devyn was saying. "Vaughn and I had a bet that you'd be back in Washington before Labor Day."

"You both lost that bet. Feel free to send me the money."

"It wasn't a *money* kind of bet, Sydney," Devyn said with a laugh.

There was no reason that should annoy her either. Sydney loved her sister and she was a huge fan of Vaughn's, too. She'd liked him when they'd been step-siblings and she loved him with Devyn.

And yet.

"I'm glad that I can provide entertainment from over a

thousand miles away."

"I'm not criticizing you," her older sister replied immediately, in that knowing way she had, as if she could see inside Sydney. When Sydney had always preferred that no one look at her too closely. "I'm only pointing out that this is a departure for you."

"But here's the thing, Devyn," Sydney said, rocking to a stop on the sidewalk, trying to lose herself in the glare of the bunting festooned all over the local drugstore. "Maybe it's not a departure. Maybe I've been trying to come back to Marietta my whole life, but I didn't know how."

"You have been going back to Marietta your whole life. And then leaving again, as quickly as possible."

Sydney didn't think she'd ever *ground* her teeth together the way she did then.

"Things are different now," she managed to grit out from between clenched teeth. "Yes, I'm on a leave of absence, but also it feels like Grandma and Grandpa need me. Or they need someone, anyway." She thought of Skylar's calm admonishment, and agreed. "There's too much squabbling and carrying on and none of it has much to do with the two elderly people who need to be taken care of whether they like it or not."

"Because that goes over so well in our family. Forcing care upon those who don't want it."

"They're stubborn," Sydney said, just as she'd said to her uncles this morning. "But there's a fine line between good, old-fashioned Montana stubborn and just plain foolish, and I want to make sure we're all on the right side of that divide."

There was a pause, and Sydney knew her sister well enough for that pause to put her on high alert.

"And none of this has to do with a certain ridiculously hot cowboy that Luce says you've been spending time with?" Devyn asked, with studied nonchalance Sydney didn't think either one of them believed.

But at least the change of subject got them away from what felt a lot like an attack on her ability to be something other than the flake her sister thought she was. Her jaw was starting to ache.

"I don't know what that would have to do with anything," Sydney replied primly. "I've known Jackson for a long time. He's… He's just…"

But her tongue didn't seem to work. Because Jackson wasn't *just* anything. And she had a terrible fear that if she said it out loud—if she actually said out loud what that tangled little thread of hope suggested he was—

She couldn't. That was the beginning and the end of it. She *couldn't.*

"He's fun," she said instead.

And hated herself.

"I've never known you to do any of these things," her sister said after a moment. A moment during which Sydney could both imagine the expression on her face and was glad she couldn't see it. She was afraid it would make her cry, and she didn't want to examine *that* at all. "I applaud it all."

"I'm glad it makes you feel like applauding," Sydney muttered. "Like a game show."

And after she hung up, she realized she'd been too busy acting like a surly thirteen-year-old to ask Devyn what she meant. What, exactly, she'd never known Sydney to do. Did she mean Sydney didn't have fun? Or that she didn't typically deal with her family without always having a screen in the way?

Both, in all likelihood. She could admit that.

Because the truth was, she really didn't do either of those things too often and she never had. Her mother had been more than enough family for anyone, and, of course, her father had his own family. And now Devyn had her own family too. Like all the rest of her cousins did, or planned to.

Meanwhile Sydney had what she'd always had. All-consuming work and the community of people she saw there, wafting about like ghosts in a machine at all hours of the day and night, passing in hallways and nodding over their laptops to each other during meetings—

She pushed through the doors into Grey's Saloon with the sort of energy that might have gotten a gunslinger in trouble back in the day. Her uncle looked up from the bar and frowned, but she wasn't worried about Jason. She was hit with the music from the jukebox, the sound of pool cues hitting balls, and the chatter of people who looked like they wanted to be exactly where they were.

And she didn't feel like a ghost at all as she walked inside, took her place behind the bar, and lost herself in the usual dance of slinging drinks for these people she was already coming to know. She liked the banter, which nobody got from Jason, but which Sydney found she was happy to give to whoever happened to place an order. Reese Kendrick, Jason's heir apparent even though Jason himself would likely die on a barstool here, was equally laconic. Sydney liked taking up the slack. She liked learning the locals' names, their drinks, and even thought it was fun to provide some comic relief, depending on the moment.

*See, Devyn,* she said in her head. *I'm a freaking delight.*

Then again, maybe what she liked best of all was glancing over every time she heard the door open, waiting for the moment when it would be Jackson who walked in.

Because when he did, just like always, she felt him.

Everywhere.

And it was a different kind of feeling, after spending time here. After spending time with him. After the conversations they'd had about his childhood in Texas. About the grandparents he adored and the mother he would always mourn. About how different their childhoods had been, and what that meant. How it had formed them each so differently, and yet here they were, tangled up in each other for all these years.

The thing about Jackson was that it was easy to talk to him.

When the only thing Sydney had ever found easy before him was data.

He took his time coming over to the bar, and there was no longer any pretending that he wasn't headed straight for her. She found she could hardly remember the person she'd been, the one who'd taken such pleasure in playing games like that.

Today he took his time because he had so many people to speak to. A handshake here, a shoulder clapped there. Everyone in town knew him. It looked like most of them liked him.

It was kind of funny how much Sydney liked that, too. When she knew what she knew about city people and their longing for anonymity because she'd been that city person. For years and years.

"Afternoon, darlin'," Jackson drawled when he met her on the other side of the bar. They grinned at each other, with all that polished wood in between them and Morgan Wallen singing about complicated nights in the background. "I'm headed over to FlintWorks."

It gave her a little thrill that she could decode that sentence without asking for details. She knew what he meant was that he was going into work, but had come to find her first. And that he hadn't come here because he wanted a drink or to play pool or even to flirt with her in the hope that she would turn up later. He had things to do that would require he use his brain. And yes, he lived right next to his business. So he had taken the time to come over this way, because he, like her, was getting into the habit of this.

The habit of them.

"Maybe I'll come by later," Sydney said, and now her jaw ached from smiling so wide. "When my shift is over."

"Make it a plan," he returned, that banked fire forever in his gaze. "Not a maybe. I'll make dinner."

And she didn't point out that this could easily have been a phone call. A text. Because she liked it too, this getting to see him when she didn't expect it. Getting to take advantage of the fact that they not only both lived in this town, but were currently living in a manner that allowed them to see each other this often.

She didn't have to have dated a ton of people before this to know that it was a gift. And unusual.

And yet another benefit of this small-town thing.

"That sounds perfect," she said, because she was a girl dating a guy in a small town, and he was going to feed her. Talk to her. Listen to her. Then, knowing him, walk her home. And if there was something more perfect than that, she couldn't imagine it. "I'll bring dessert."

Jackson grinned at her in that way she knew was only hers. "You know I have a sweet tooth," he drawled. "But you could also just bring you."

And Sydney was humming a little bit under her breath long after he'd gone.

Maybe more than a little bit.

At the end of her shift, she went to the back office. Jason was sitting behind his desk, scowling at a stack of papers. Or at the desk itself, it was hard to tell.

It being Jason, it was possible that he wasn't scowling at all. Sydney had long wondered if Grandma's warnings had come true after all and his face had gotten stuck that way.

"I can't tell if you're angry about something new," she said, in the bright voice she knew made Jason marginally apoplectic. And it was less *marginal* all the time. "But I've been meaning to tell you that, personally, I think it's a good thing that so many members of the family want to be involved in Grandma and Grandpa's next steps. We definitely weren't always so aligned."

He lifted that scowl her way and rubbed at his forehead like she was giving him a headache. "Who died and made you little Miss Mary Sunshine?"

Sydney ignored that. And also the fact that this was now a second family member who assumed a whole death was necessary to explain her behavior. Behavior that she didn't think was particularly noteworthy or dramatic. "Surely the entire point of family is to rally around things exactly like this."

"Is that what you think they're doing? Because to me it sounds like a whole lot of people who don't have to deal with the fallout of any decisions that are made here, shooting their mouths off from afar."

"A bunch of people are shooting their mouths off right

here in town," she countered. Because no one had to die to make her mouthy. It was just that she usually didn't think it was worth it to get mouthy around her family.

Jason wasn't frowning at her any longer. And yet, somehow, the look he leveled on her was far darker. "I've known my parents longer than you have, Sydney. You might want to remember that."

Sydney sighed. She reached up to pull her hair out of its ponytail, the one she always wore to keep it out of the drinks. "I know you have. And I'm not trying to contradict you or fight with you. It's just..." She shook her head. "Do you know, I really think Grandpa just wants to be wherever Grandma is. I don't think this is going to be the fight you imagine. Not if we figure out how to make it seem like it's her decision. Right?"

And that glimmering thread of hope inside her seemed to loop around a time or two more.

Jason studied her for a long moment, and something in her chest clutched a bit when she realized the way he was looking at her looked a lot like... pity.

But that couldn't be right.

"Didn't anyone ever tell you that misery loves company?" he asked quietly.

"I've heard that," she replied, her spine stiffening of its own accord. "But here you are, all alone."

His mouth curved a little at that hit, but he didn't react. Not the way she wanted him to, anyway. "My parents are not happy people. They weren't happy parents and they aren't happy grandparents, in case you haven't noticed. Maybe we shouldn't listen to them about what it would take for them to achieve a state they've never, ever enjoyed."

"Uncle Jason. I love you. But how would you know the difference?" He scowled again and started to speak, but she continued. "I'm being serious. I'm not trying to be mean. But how would you, specifically, know the difference?"

It was silent between them, and it was strange, this whole being an adult thing. Because she could remember all too well the many, many years she'd been a kid, and he'd been so much more grown-up not only than her, but older than her mother as well. Always an adult. Always right simply because of that.

But she wasn't a kid anymore. They were both adults. That meant she could talk to him the way she would to any other adult she knew. No matter how strange it felt.

And it was more than strange, with his personal history stretched out there between them, then. The wife who'd left him so long ago now, the daughters who'd mostly followed suit. He was the loneliest man she knew.

She had always thought he took a kind of pleasure in that. Or at least some measure of satisfaction.

But there didn't seem to be any kind of pleasure in him now. And no hint of anything like satisfaction. He looked at her and it was clear that he, too, was seeing the same kinds of ghosts that she was. And maybe the specter of the fact that she was no kid anymore, either.

"I'm sorry," Sydney said quietly. "I wasn't trying to be mean. Really."

"I'm going to do you the same courtesy," Jason said. And something more than just her spine stiffened at that. At the way he looked at her, his gaze steady. Direct. She braced herself. "You're not going to stay here, Sydney. You know it. I know it. Everyone else in the family certainly knows it. There's only one person in Marietta who doesn't know it, isn't there."

It was such an unexpected sort of collision. Everything inside her seem to buckle at that. She couldn't breathe, it was such a sucker punch. The fact that she was still standing came as a surprise.

"And I might be miserable," he said in that same low voice. "Sometimes I even revel in it. That doesn't keep me from understanding that you're going to break that poor man in half. Because when you go back home, he's going to stay here. Just as miserable as me." He smiled again, and this time, she thought it broke something inside of her. Because it was nothing but a reflection of what little in him wasn't broken already. "A fate worse than death, some might say. Is that what you want for Jackson?"

# Chapter Eight

IT WAS HARDER to get away from the brewery than he expected that night. The rodeo was finally here and the town was hopping, so Jackson worked straight up to closing time. This was earlier for FlintWorks than the other bars in town, but that just meant they started on the cleanup earlier too.

Because they'd had such a banner turnout, all Copper Mountain Rodeo folks and fans, it made sense for him to help after they closed, too. He wasn't the kind of boss who expected his employees to do anything he wouldn't, and tonight was no time to change course.

It was only when he was locking up that it occurred to him that Sydney should have showed by now.

But then, even as he was completing that thought, he saw her. She was sitting on the steps of the old depot, her elbows on her knees and her hair all around her face like a curtain.

He could see that something was wrong. He could feel it. She didn't look up as he came closer. She didn't give him that smile of hers that he'd come to depend upon.

Jackson hadn't known just how much he'd depended on

it until now, when it was nowhere to be found.

"You should have gone inside," he told her as he walked toward the steps. "You know I don't lock the door."

And if things were all right, she would have made one of her usual cracks about how different things were here than back in DC. She would have shuddered theatrically, making it clear that she did not have the trusting ways of country folk.

There'd been a time when she'd meant it when she said things like that. Lately, she said them with that little smile of hers that made him think she liked being one of those country folk herself.

But tonight, she didn't react. She didn't look up.

"Jackson," she said, though she was talking to her knees. "We have to talk."

"Great," he replied. "I'm all for talking. Seems to me, I'm the one who's been on the side of talking all along."

She sat back and looked up then, and he froze, because he hadn't seen this expression on her face in a long, long while.

"We have to break up," she told him, in the kind of rush that made him think that she thought she needed to get the words out fast. Like maybe she wouldn't say them at all if she gave them time to marinate. "And I know we're not really together, that this is just dating—"

"Sydney. Baby. Nothing between us is *just* anything."

She shot up to her feet then, with all that agitation that

he could feel inside him, too, until she was vibrating there before him. Right there and yet completely out of reach. "I know you're not going to believe this, but it's for your own good," she said, as if the words cut her tongue on their way out.

"You're right." He sounded flat. Hard. He felt… well. There was no name for it, but it was harsh and wild and he wasn't sure he had complete control of it. "I don't believe it."

"You're not the only one who can be noble, you know." But that came out less like a rush or an agitated vibration and more like a plea. Then she lifted her hands, as if in supplication, and she was killing him. "How is this going to end, Jackson? What's going to happen?"

"I have a lot of thoughts about that, as a matter fact." He moved closer, more to get on the same rise and fall of breath than to touch her. But her eyes were dark. And her arms were folded in front of her. And she danced back, out of reach, and killed him all over again. But that didn't stop him. "It might surprise you to learn that I've given it a lot of thought. I'm not worried, darlin'. One way or the other, we'll work it out."

"But it's going to be *work*." And he couldn't say he liked the way she said that. Particularly that word. "Best case scenario, worst case scenario, it's still going to be work. And I already have a job that takes up every single ounce of time I have. You know this. So walk me through how you think it's going to go." She blew out a breath, ruffling her bangs. "I go back to DC. And we… What? Text? Try to grab a phone call when we can? I can tell you right now, I'm going to let you down."

"Sydney—"

"It's inevitable. I won't even mean it. But I will. I'll do it slowly, over time, so that even the memory of this is ruined. That's what's going to happen."

"That sounds like a whole lot of weight to put on something we don't have to worry about yet," he said, and he was glad of every moment in his life that had taught him how to be calm under pressure. Because it had never mattered more than it did now. "Another option is that we could… see what happens. Maybe it won't be what you think. Maybe you'll stay. Maybe I'll move to DC. We have months to decide. It seems to me that you want to throw in the towel now because you're afraid."

"I am afraid," she threw back at him. "For you."

"For me," Jackson repeated, getting a little bit lost in his drawl. "You have to help me out here. What makes you think that I need you to be afraid for me?" He wasn't getting mad, not exactly. But it was more difficult to keep himself calm than anything had been before. Ever. "I thought you knew this about me. I'm pretty damn good at beating the odds."

"These aren't the kind of odds you're used to," Sydney threw back at him. She shoved a hand through her hair, another sign of agitation he really wished she'd let him soothe away. "It's really nice that so many members of my family have somehow gotten over their stuff and found a way to be happy. That's what they say they are, anyway and there's a lot about coming back to Marietta it makes me imagine I could be happy too. But then I look at the truth of things. Not what I want, but what *is*. And I have to analyze it with my head, not my heart."

Jackson didn't think this was the right time to feel triumphant that she would mention her heart at all. But it was a victory all the same.

"My grandfather seems to think that it's worth a lifetime of bitterness for just a couple of moments of something sweet," she was saying, her eyes wide like she was looking at a nightmare. Or she was seeing the two of them starring in one. "My mother has always believed that chasing her own happiness was more important than anything else. Her children. Her life. Every single promise she ever made. But at the end of the day, they've mostly been miserable. Just like my uncle Jason is miserable. And lonely. And why? Because they don't learn. They're still trying to do the very thing they already know they can't, because they've failed time and time and time again. But I don't need to subject myself to this."

"To this," he repeated. "You mean, to me."

"I don't mean that," she said thickly, and it wasn't that he liked the sound of tears in her voice. But he found a little solace that this wasn't easy for her. And maybe that was all he was going to get, so he figured he'd take it. "Or not exactly."

And he wanted to jump in. He wanted to argue. He

wanted to fight—but he didn't.

Because he couldn't fight the ghosts inside of her. Only she could do that. Everything else was yelling.

And worse, might just prove her point.

She made a low sort of noise, close but not quite a sob. "Jackson. When I'm at work, nothing else exists. Nothing else matters. I like it that way."

"Sydney," he replied, in the exact same tone, "breaking up with me isn't going to make me stop loving you. Whether I exist to you while you're at work or not. You know that, right?"

And she gasped a little at that. Like he'd hauled off and hit her.

Jackson decided that maybe it was okay to mix it up a little. "I love you," he told her, in a voice that brooked no opposition. He could see the way it settled in on her. And the way she shuddered, like it was taking root and she didn't quite know what to do with it. "And I know that's terrifying. But there's no other word that fits, and I think you know it. But love doesn't have to follow a script. It doesn't even have to feel good all the time, because sometimes it's more complicated than that. What I know about love isn't all puppies and rainbows. It's how I lost my mother, how I held her hand while she slipped away. How my grandparents stood by me, and said goodbye to their child. It's the way my brothers welcomed me into the family when they could easily have turned their backs. And it's you."

She shook her head, but her eyes were too bright with tears, and though her throat worked, no words came out.

So he kept going. "It's how I took one look at you outside, with a snowstorm coming in, and wasn't cold anymore. It's how I knew in that moment that nothing would ever be the same. And baby. It hasn't."

"You want that to be true," she managed to say then, though her voice was ragged and she seemed a little too close to toppling over for his peace of mind. "You want it all to come together and make some kind of pretty story, but it doesn't. Not for me. This is what I've been trying to tell you all along." She took a hand and circled it over her torso. "That thing inside? I don't have it."

She looked so defiant and so lost, and he thought that he had never loved her more.

"It's your heart, Sydney," he replied gently. "And I can feel it beating every time I touch you. I can feel it against mine. I can feel it in your pulse. I can hear it in the way you breathe. You might not be able to feel it yourself, but I know it's there."

But she was shaking her head again, and took another step back—only to come up against the wall of the train depot. She made a frustrated sound.

"I've done this analysis again and again," she told him. "It doesn't make sense. Love sometimes works, for some people, but all the rest of the time? It devastates. We have weapons that do less damage. There are casualties either way but with love? They just… walk around. They walk and talk and pretend they're alive. I should have known better. I did know better, watching the way my mother let love trample all over her all my life. But I wanted…"

"Me," he supplied. "You wanted me. And do you want to know why?"

"Because I'm just as bad as my mother," she said stoutly, definitively, but there was that hitch in her voice. "I want things I shouldn't and then I can't understand why they hurt. It's the family curse. I keep trying—"

"Baby, you're in love with me," Jackson said. And while he didn't feel *calm*, not really, he no longer felt close to losing it, either. Because this was no more and no less than the truth. This was the truest thing he knew, and it was almost peaceful to say it, even in a moment like this one. Because she wouldn't, and it needed to be spoken out loud. "If I had to guess, it hit you at first sight too. And we've both been grappling with that ever since. But you hid behind the distance. And I let you. That's not going to happen anymore."

"It's not going to happen at all," she said, but to his ear, she was starting to sound… desperate. Determined. But certainly not filled with anything like the quiet, certain ring of truth.

At least he had that going for him.

"I don't like to brag," he told her then. "But it's not like I'm stuck here. If I need to remove distance as a stumbling block, I'm happy to do it." He watched her blink at that, as if it hadn't occurred to him that he really could do just that. He could call her bluff just as easily in the nation's capital as he could here. So he pressed the issue. "Because I don't see the point of being alive if we don't give things like this the chance they deserve. Isn't this the whole reason we're here?"

And he knew—he could see—that at last he'd hit his target.

That heart she thought she didn't have.

But he wasn't surprised that her response was to back away, her eyes full of tears. He doubted she would admit that that's what they were, but he could see the soft, sad shine.

When she spoke, she had put more distance between them, but he could hear the raggedness of her voice just fine. "I don't know why we're here. And I really don't know why I'm *here*, in Marietta, when I could be anywhere. I don't know what I was thinking."

"You were thinking it was time to come home," he said quietly. With great deliberation and his eyes on hers. "And Sydney. It is. I promise you, it is."

But she was already making a break for it and he knew he had to let her do it. Because it didn't matter how true this was, this thing between them.

If she didn't want it. If she wouldn't acknowledge it.

Then again, a man didn't become a professional athlete, then retire on his own terms, without knowing a tactic or two.

"I'm not going to bring this up again or push you," he told her as she kept inching backward as if waiting for the right moment to turn and run. "But remember, you promised me a dance."

If he'd said that he wanted her to find a pony and canter straight on up toward the moon, he doubted she could have looked more floored. Her mouth actually dropped open. "What?"

"A dance," he said patiently. "You promised right here on this stoop. You read that very poster, and told me you never danced with a man before. Certainly not on a date."

For a moment she only stared back at him. Then her mouth snapped shut. She looked past him at the poster for the rodeo that hung there, listing out all the events. One of them being tomorrow's barbecue on Main Street that so many people looked forward to, followed by dancing right there in the closed-off street. Where, if the stories he'd heard were true, his own brother Jasper had once declared his intentions to his Mayor Chelsea, right out there in front of everybody.

When Sydney looked back at him, she was shaking her head, which surprised him not at all. "When I agreed to that I wasn't in my right mind. Obviously."

"It will be fun. We can have fun, can't we?"

He tucked it away, the guilty way she reacted to that. He would have to look at it later. Think about why the word *fun* would make her look… something like ashamed.

And for a moment he saw his Sydney there, beneath the storm that she'd come to him with tonight. "It's been pointed out to me that I don't know how to be fun. Or have it. Or be adjacent to it in any regard."

Jackson inclined his head at that. He even tipped his hat, like the courtly old cowboy his grandfather expected him to become. "Well, darlin', it will be my pleasure to show you." And when she started to protest, he shook his head, and smiled. Because he knew she couldn't resist. He was counting on it. "I insist."

# Chapter Nine

SYDNEY SPENT THE whole next day assuring herself that she was absolutely, positively, not showing up for anything like a *dance*. No matter what she might have promised while all hopped up on *dating* and *kissing*.

She was sure that Jackson was going to try to change her mind, and she'd marched all the way back to the Graff in the dark, muttering to herself out loud that she couldn't let him. That she *wouldn't* let him. That Uncle Jason had said his piece and she'd listened and that was that. It would be painful—it was already so painful she almost wondered if she'd broken a rib without noticing it—

But she didn't sleep well. Maybe she didn't sleep at all. Then again, she must have slept a little, because all she could see were images of Jackson in her head. And all she could do was replay that conversation over and over and over.

Like it was still happening, and then it was morning.

*I love you,* he'd said.

*You're in love with me,* he'd said.

And the heart she'd claimed she didn't have beat so hard against her broken ribs that she was sure it was leaving bruises. Deep inside, but she could feel them every time she moved. Every time she breathed.

Every second, and she was afraid they were getting bigger.

"I am *definitely* not going to any *dance*," she told the ceiling of her hotel room.

But the day wore on. There were too many conversations with her cousins, all of them with a whole lot of opinions, and not one of them sounding even remotely miserable.

Like it was easy.

Even for her mother.

"Of course my brothers are fighting," Melody said with a laugh. "You can be sure that Billy would be fighting too but he likes to play power games, which in his case mostly means he pretends not to be involved. Like Billings is on a different planet instead of in the same state. I wouldn't be surprised if he swooped in at the last minute, and personally relocated Mom and Dad himself."

"I'll pass that along," Sydney said.

Admittedly, she sounded a little grumpy. More than *a little* grumpy, in the spirit of total honesty.

Melody let out that laugh of hers that Sydney had heard more than one former suitor of hers refer to as the *very sound of sunshine*.

And maybe it was. One thing Sydney knew about sunshine was that it burned. You could pretend it didn't. You could prance around talking about primal forces and vitamin D and end up with burned skin all the same.

She did not share these thoughts with her mother. Or her *sunshiny* laugh.

"Is Marietta getting to you?" Melody asked when the laughter ebbed. "I thought it might. Remember, I grew up there."

"I love the town, actually," Sydney said at once, and, sure, a little aggressively. "If you think about it, it's really the only touchstone I've ever had. Thanks to all those summers you left me here. I like to think of it as home, Mom."

"Home but not really," her mother replied, seemingly airily unaware of Sydney's tone. A maddening tactic she'd always used that never got any less maddening, it turned out. Even if, despite herself, Sydney was forced to think about useful that tactic must have been growing up with Elly and Richard and all those uncles, not a soft personality to be found among the lot of them. "All the nostalgia and none of the commitment."

Sydney was furious that she'd almost felt sympathy for Melody. More than that, she felt a little dizzy, standing there in nothing but her underwear in her room in the Graff. As if the earthquakes rolling one into the next inside of her might tip her straight over—

Or maybe she was just holding her breath.

Testing that theory, she took a deep breath. Then another. And her temper didn't go anywhere, but sure enough, the dizziness eased.

*Damn it.*

"I'm glad that everything's ended well for you and Derrick," she managed to say. "But as one of the people who had to put up with a lot of the roads you took on your way to ending well? I'm here to tell you that it wasn't that great of a ride."

In the past, any hint of criticism sent Melody over the edge. Tears, drama, the works.

Maybe Sydney was just childish enough today that she wanted Melody to feel as badly as she did.

She couldn't say she liked knowing that about herself.

But she also didn't take it back.

"I'm sorry about that," Melody said, quietly. Direct and to the point. No excuses. No *buts.* No unnecessary explanations or blame.

And nothing could have shocked Sydney more. The only thing she could hear in her room was her own jagged breath, and instead of singing inappropriately or laughing or screaming, her mother seemed to have gone quiet. But she was still there. Sydney could hear her. It was almost as if she was… actually contemplating what Sydney had said to her.

It made Sydney wonder if, after all this time, Melody had finally changed into that version of herself her daughters had only seen rarely. So very rarely that they'd stopped talking about it, because it was too painful.

Really it was too painful now, too.

Melody wasn't done with the surprises. "I spent half my life trying to get some kind of response from my parents, and the other half trying to get any response from anyone at all," she said. "I got lost in it. I've had half a decade to think on that now, and I know I didn't come out well. I'm sorry, Sydney. I am. If that helps."

It was the way she said that. It made Sydney think of her new husband, Derrick Voss, Devyn's father. Who everyone seemed to agree was her last husband. Because the man didn't play. And he wasn't lost.

What she remembered from him was all granite and steel and *certainty*.

Sydney felt as if she could hear a little of that in her mother's voice.

And that voice inside her, that jerk of a voice, chose that moment to pipe up. *Maybe what you've called working was nothing but getting lost all along.*

"I guess that's nice to hear," she managed to say to her mother, though she was feeling like too many earthquakes again. "I'm afraid that doesn't solve any of my problems. One of them being grandparents who apparently want to die on their own in Big Sky out of sheer stubbornness. Another one being all the members of the family who keep calling me to tell me what I should do because I happen to be here. Oh, and let's not forget, the eternal problem that's just... me."

This time when Melody laughed, it made something inside Sydney seem to lurch to one side, like something critical had broken loose.

"You have always been the funniest girl," Melody told

her, with a kindness and a warmth in her voice that made Sydney's eyes sting. "So serious. So stern, especially when you were small. When you started eating with utensils, you took offense against it if anyone made noise in the room while you were trying to eat. We all had to sit quietly, respectfully, and wait for you to finish."

"I don't know what to do with that anecdote."

"You don't have to do anything with it, my dear, sweet, fury of a daughter," Melody replied. "But I'll ask you this. Do you still require that everybody in the vicinity quiet down just because you decided to eat something?"

"Obviously not."

"The thing to remember, to hold to if you can, is that everything changes." Melody sounded almost sad. Or maybe she sounded… open and vulnerable, and what was Sydney supposed to do with *that*? "The question is, can you change too? Or are you too busy trying to hold onto something that only worked in the first place because the people who loved you let it?"

And then, because she was still maddening in every regard no matter how much her marriage and supposed happiness was changing her, Melody hung up.

Sydney threw her phone onto the bed with more force than was necessary. And then stood there, fuming.

And still in nothing but her underwear.

"This all has to stop," she told herself in the mirror. "You have to go. Now."

But when the phone rang again, it was Aunt Gracie. And before Sydney knew it, she agreed to go and pick up Elly and Richard so they could stay in Gracie and Ryan's spare room for the weekend, and do the rodeo thing.

"And, hopefully, we can convince them to stay," Gracie said.

Sydney still had no intention of going to the dance, and now she had a good reason for it. She was taking care of her *elderly grandparents.* She couldn't concern herself with such *frivolity.*

*Because they'll accept a nursemaid, suddenly,* came that voice. *And even if they would, why would it be you? You do computers, not people.*

"Shut up," Sydney told herself.

In the lobby, sadly, where a surprised middle-aged couple looked at her like she was a monster as she walked by, seemingly telling them to shut up.

She drove all the way out to Big Sky in the same rush of what she refused to call temper—or something stickier and more upsetting, like fear. She corralled said elderly grandparents and got them into the car, though it would have been easier to herd up a platoon or two of feral cats. Then she drove back to Marietta while her grandmother critiqued her driving and her grandfather kept messing with the car radio, looking for what he called the right and proper country music of his youth.

He didn't find it.

Sydney had been very clear that she had no intention of involving herself with anything Marietta, her family, the Copper Mountain Rodeo, or dancing dates with Jackson. But then, despite herself, there she was. Walking down Main Street as dusk settled in and it was transformed into something magical all around her.

Main Street, Marietta, was already magical. She'd accepted that a long time ago. It was magical in the dark of winter and at high noon on a summer's day.

But tonight all the banners proclaimed the 85th Copper Mountain Rodeo. Lights were strung to stretch from one side of the street to the other. The whole street was blocked off and there was even a stage at one end, where a band was playing exactly the kind of music Grandpa liked.

But somehow she couldn't make herself leave.

Sydney escorted Elly and Richard to one of the tables set up for the older folks. She told herself that she was heartless. That she was an android, as accused. That she was in no way *lost* in the job that she had *chosen*—

Well, she thought, before that voice inside of her could kick in. She hadn't actually *chosen* the job, had she? They had chosen her. And it had seemed so exciting, after the benign neglect of her mother and her father's distance and disinterest, to be unequivocally wanted. To have people pursue her, telling her that she was smart and perfect for the job, and would be an asset to the department.

Sydney liked being *an asset.*

She stared up at the fairy lights that twinkled against the dark backdrop of the night, and the Montana stars far above. And she wondered how it was possible to feel so lost and so found, all at the same time.

*You're going to have to get used to it,* she told herself, or maybe it was that same voice telling her, and suddenly the months stretching in front of her to the end of the years seemed like nothing short of a prison sentence.

She wasn't sure she could do this kind of time. Not in this town that felt like him.

And then she looked up when someone came to stand before her, and she knew that whatever she felt about fairy lights and the stars above and this happy little jewel of a town was nothing compared to the way she felt when she looked at Jackson.

He was dressed for the occasion in his best jeans, showy boots to announce the Texas in him, and a very nice shirt he'd tucked in behind the kind of buckle some men competed for. Not that Jackson had to compete. He tipped his Stetson to her and made her wish she'd put on something a lot nicer—or a lot more revealing—than the sundress she was wearing purely to avoid her grandmother's commentary on *girls these days*, and a pair of flats.

But she felt that she was wearing some kind of epic ball gown when he put out his hand, that mouth of his so beautiful and so unsmiling, and waited for her to take it.

She knew she shouldn't—but maybe that had been a lie

all along. Just fear talking, and that controlling creature she'd always been inside, apparently, even when she was a toddler.

Because despite the turmoil inside of her, all she did—all she wanted to do—was slip her hand into his.

She heard her grandmother say something, but it was lost in the whirl of the music playing and the crowd all around them.

And for once in her life, Sydney didn't think.

She didn't analyze, she didn't arrange the data before her and try to draw conclusions.

She simply wrapped her arms around Jackson's neck and danced with him.

Around and around and around, until the lights felt like they gleamed inside of her, a part of that jagged ache. Until she felt bruised inside and out.

Or maybe she meant tender. She danced with him and she felt *tender*.

One song ended and another began, and she should have pulled away, but she didn't.

And it was hard to say how much time had passed. There was nothing for her but his arms around her. His gaze on hers like a promise. Like its own *I love you*. There was nothing but Jackson until the band put down their instruments to take a break, and various folks began making speeches.

Sydney knew she had no more excuse to stand there, holding on to Jackson the way she was.

She made herself step back. She made herself look at him, too. Because once upon a time, she'd been known for her ability to shoot from the hip and get straight to the point.

Everything since then, she thought now, was an anomaly.

Or so she told herself, by all the light of a Copper Mountain Rodeo evening with Jackson Flint watching her like she was the only thing he planned to look at forever.

"Baby," he began, that light in his gaze.

But the beauty of a crowd, Sydney discovered, was that she could use the crush of people to put distance between her and this conversation she didn't want to have. She could tell herself that the bruised and aching thing inside of her was telling her to get away from him, even though it was clear that every step she took in the opposite direction made it hurt worse.

She could tell herself anything and she did, weaving her way through the groups of happy, laughing people standing up and sitting at the tables and set out on the street, until she found her grandparents once again.

It was almost comforting that they were sitting there in silence, engaged once again in that cold war of theirs. Anyway, it felt normal when nothing else did.

Maybe if she watched their deep chill long enough, she'd learn how to do it.

Maybe if she really studied them, she could get that grim

inside, too.

But something of what she was feeling must have showed on her face. She thought that she knew better than that. She should, by now. Yet when she looked up from an intense examination of the hands that had last pressed against Jackson's body it was to find her grandmother watching her with a sour look on her face.

"I keep trying to tell you," Elly said with a sniff. "It's the blood. It's cursed."

"I don't know what you mean," Sydney lied. And she shook her head, horrified to discover that when she did, she could feel too much moisture in the back of her eyes. As if everything tonight was conspiring to give her away.

*Or,* came that voice, *is it possible you're finally tired of all these lies you tell yourself?*

And it was that moment when she realized whose voice that was. Whose voice it had always been. It was her.

It was her, but it wasn't the Sydney she'd been for all these years now. Not the Sydney her grandmother seemed to think she was speaking to now, frowning at her from across the table while the crowd milled all around them.

It was partly the Sydney who'd gone on those dates with Jackson. It was partly the Sydney who had looked at him outside that bar, so long ago now, and had known, deep down in a place she'd never looked at again, that she was done.

That Sydney had been here, all along, just waiting for her

to notice herself again.

And it didn't feel like an earthquake to recognize herself.

It felt like a key in a lock.

"I saw that cowboy come over here," Elly was saying, in her usual way. "You could hardly miss him. He has the look of those brothers of his, and I hate to tell you this, Sydney, but you need to be careful. Two Flint brothers might have settled down, but you can be sure that this one, with his flashy past is the one who's going to turn out bad. He's the one who's going to make you wish you'd looked in the other direction while you still could." She sniffed in her longsuffering way. "And believe me when I tell you that you don't want to spend all the years that I have, suffering for one bad decision."

And Sydney was generally of the opinion that there was no purpose in arguing with a nearly ninety-year-old woman. Talk about your Pyrrhic victories, assuming there was even something to be won.

But tonight it seemed that other Sydney had the wheel.

Because she didn't just sigh and change the subject. She didn't roll her eyes, then get up to call a cousin and complain. She didn't murmur some platitude, so that Elly would turn that fierce attention of hers elsewhere.

Instead, she sat forward. She leaned her elbows on the table, held her grandmother's gaze, and for the first time in her entire life, confronted this particular problem instead of running away from it.

So in that sense it was a victory before she said a single word.

But she intended to say more than one. "Has it ever occurred to you, Grandma, that you're not suffering for any reason except that you choose to?" Her grandmother sputtered, but Sydney didn't stop. "I spent my whole life thinking that your heart was cold, and how could you help that? I thought that's why you couldn't see that all the people around you were trying their best to love you. But you do see, don't you?"

Her grandmother stared back at her, and it was like looking in that mirror in the Graff again. They were too much alike. Maybe that was the trouble.

And if this was where Sydney was headed, she wanted no part of it.

"Maybe it's not that your heart is cold, but that it's broken," she continued, because she had to continue or die. It felt that stark. "It's broken and it's been broken for decades, and despite taking so much pride in all your pioneer ways, you don't know how to put it back together."

"You have no idea what you're talking about, child," Grandma said, but she was looking at Sydney as if she was looking at a ghost.

Maybe they were haunting each other.

"I know exactly what I'm talking about, actually," Sydney replied. "Because I've been trying my best to be you and I didn't even realize it. I've been shutting myself down, turning myself off, just taking it as a fact with no proof whatsoever that I'm as ruined as you are. When I don't want to be."

She said that again, internally, so it had a chance in hell of sticking. *I don't want to be ruined.*

Elly stared back at her, all but trembling with affront. "This is how you treat your grandmother?"

"I'm more interested in how you've always spoken to all of us," Sydney replied, not unkindly. Because she wasn't mad. This wasn't an earthquake. She wasn't trembling. She was just… sad, she supposed. For Elly. For herself. For all of them, from Uncle Jason on down across all these years. "All the terrible tales you told us about what we could expect, and who we would turn out to be, like it or not. All this talk of curses. And all the ways you showed us, over and over again, that forgiveness was never an option. That no one could ever be good enough and no apology could ever fix it or offer any shot at redemption. That it was more important to make someone pay for your hurt feelings than to try to fix yourself. Grow. Or change in any way." She stopped to take a breath, aware that she could feel her heart beating in her ears. Her wrists. And it wasn't because she was out of control or in a panic. It was her heart, beating. Reminding her that she was alive and she was here and she wasn't anyone but herself. She could change any part of her that she liked. Maybe that was even the point. "That's what you taught me, Grandma. And look at me. I'm your best and brightest student."

Both of her grandparents were staring back at her, and Sydney imagined that at some point, she would feel badly about this. But not right now.

Right now she felt like she'd been waiting to say these things her whole life. Or, more than that, she'd been waiting to be the person who could say them.

Because no one else in her family could. Or would.

She didn't remember getting to her feet but there she was, standing there with her hands flat on the table so she could look them both in the face.

"I don't want to spend even one moment walking around with broken pieces inside of me," Sydney said, with a kind of certainty she wasn't sure she'd ever felt before. "Much less seventy years. I don't want to be broken. I don't want to *feel* broken. I want to feel alive, Grandma. And it makes me desperately sad to know that you never have. Not really."

Maybe that was too far. Sydney knew that she should feel ashamed, and if she did, it was because she was going to have to explain to her entire extended family why she'd thought it was a good idea to rant directly into her grandparents' faces.

Though, she knew that even if they all spent days calling to chide her for this, she wouldn't take a single one of the things she'd said back.

But while she was gearing up to apologize for her delivery, Grandpa got to his feet.

It took him a minute, and the help of the table and the

chair he'd been sitting in, but he managed it. He looked at Sydney and nodded, then tipped his own Stetson in her direction, like the old cowboy he was and had been for as long as she could remember.

Then he turned and looked down at Elly.

"Woman," he said, his voice gruff, "we don't have a lot of years left. Let's make them soft."

Her grandmother looked frozen. Her hands moved, and Sydney braced herself, thinking that she would try to swat Grandpa away, or throw over the table. Something big and unexpected—but instead, her hand ended up at her throat.

It had to be the softest thing Sydney had ever seen her do.

"Elly," her grandfather said in a rumbly voice that she couldn't believe was his. "My ornery love, it's time to come on home."

Then, as Sydney stared in astonishment and Jackson's similar words echoed inside of her, Grandma clambered up from her chair. She drew herself up to her tiny little height, and met Richard's gaze.

Fully.

And while Sydney held her breath, and Grandpa stared down at his wife with an intensity that made something inside Sydney shiver, Elly nodded.

Once. Then again.

And, together, they walked out as the band began playing again, and danced. Until Sydney was having trouble telling the difference between the grandparents she knew and recognized, and that picture she had in her head and on her phone.

Possibly, she thought a moment later, that was because she was well and truly crying.

And because everything was inside out tonight, she let herself. She let it go on a while. Then, when she was done, she wiped at her eyes and looked around Main Street, Marietta, the scene of miracles impossible, coming true while she watched.

She took a deep breath. She stood tall, as tall as she could.

And it was taller than her grandmother, even when Elly had been Sydney's age, because she hadn't let all the broken things take root. She hadn't let them make her someone other than who she was.

Not yet.

"Not ever," she vowed, there beneath the stars and the lights and the moon.

And then, because it was long past time, she went to find him.

To see if she really could come home.

# Chapter Ten

JACKSON SAW HER coming.

At first, he thought it was just wishful thinking, because Lord knew he was always looking for Sydney Campbell to be emerging out of his fantasies to materialize in front of him. That had been his favorite pastime for half a decade.

But his fantasies did not generally involve most of the denizens of Marietta, including everyone's favorite busybody, Carol Bingley, who was in a particularly high dither since Mayor Chelsea had seen fit to give her Marietta's Woman of the Year award. To be awarded later this very weekend.

Jackson had been sitting at the table next to Carol and her cronies, taking the opportunity to contemplate the fact that things like Woman of the Year meant different things to different people. As far as he knew, Carol Bingley had been a mainstay of the community here for as long as almost anyone could remember—like it or not.

And maybe that was a virtue in itself.

He tried to think of what his mother would say, since she'd always done her best to try to see the good in other people. He could almost hear her beside him, putting a reproving hand on his shoulder and saying something like,

*People show love in different ways, Jackson, and not all of them are comfortable. But that doesn't make it any less loving.*

He thought there was probably a reason love was on his mind.

And then Sydney was there, cutting through the crowd and heading straight for him with a look on her face that made his heart seemed to skip a beat or two inside his chest.

Maybe a whole lot more than a beat or two.

He didn't wait to see what she was coming to say to him. He was on his feet without another thought, making his way to her like she was a light in a storm.

But then, she was. She always was.

And it was almost funny that they were in the middle of a crowd, because it didn't matter. The middle of a bar, an empty street, there was only and ever Sydney.

He didn't say anything when she reached him, but when she reached out in front of her he took her hands. Then he tugged her just that little bit closer to him, so if anyone looked, it would seem as if they were dancing.

Maybe he wished they were still dancing.

"There are so many things I want to say to you," she said, tipping her head back to focus that serious, clever gaze of hers on him. With that disarming directness that had rocked him from the start. "But I don't know where to begin."

Jackson thought about all of these years. About this woman, who hid away in her data and her secrets, and showed love in one way and one way only—by showing up.

Over and over and over again.

For her family. For him.

Always.

That was how he'd known. That was how he knew now. He hadn't been the fool he'd called himself on too many dark winter nights to count—something he never questioned when she was here. In his arms, where she belonged.

He'd been right about her, and about them.

And he could see that she knew it, because it was all over her pretty face. There was that fire in her gaze that was always there—always his—but tonight it was banked by something softer. By a kind of glimmering that he could feel, inside and out.

"It's been five years already," he said, because he liked a long game, but he needed this one to end. And end right. So they could move on to the one he was certain they'd both like a whole lot better—the one they got to play together. "You can jump straight to the good part."

Assuming there was a good part. But he wasn't going to say that out loud.

And as he watched, the most beautiful smile he'd ever seen moved over her face.

He felt it everywhere.

Everywhere.

And Jackson had never spent this much time with her and not been inside her. It was a gift. It was a curse.

Right now, it felt like magic.

"Jackson," she said, as clear as a bell. "I want to come home."

"Good," he said.

Because it was. And because he wasn't sure he could get anything else out.

And it was as if the whole of Montana turned to molten gold around them. The night seemed to press in, so there were stars all over them. They danced like that with the rest of the town, promises and portents in every touch, every glance.

But she also danced with her grandfather. And Jackson danced with her grandmother, who looked at him as if she wasn't sure of him, but was surprisingly spry on her feet all the same.

When they found each other again, they were both smiling like they might never stop.

When the night was winding down and the streets of Marietta were filled with happy, content people making their way back to their homes with talk of the rodeo events the next day, Jackson helped her with her grandparents. He went with her to deliver them to her aunt and uncle, fully aware of how significant it was that she was introducing him all around like this.

"We already know Jackson," Ryan said, but the way he lifted his chin at Jackson, with a slight narrowing around the eyes, made Jackson grin. He didn't know what Stanley

Campbell was about, making Sydney feel bad somewhere in the east, but Ryan was letting him know loud and clear that she had family all the same.

He thought, when Sydney laughed at her uncle, that even she knew it.

And then, hand-in-hand, they walked down Main Street once again.

The way they'd done so many nights before.

So many cold December nights that it felt like a kind of blessing, tonight, that it was still relatively warm. But even though there were hints of fall in the cool night air, it wasn't that biting Montana winter that took no prisoners.

It was just the two of them. Him in his Stetson and fancy boots and her in a pretty dress, like they could be any cowboy and his girl on any night in the long history of this pretty little town.

Like they could be another photograph their own grandkids would find, seventy years from now, tucked away in the back of an heirloom.

He wanted it so badly he could taste it.

But first there was this. Tonight. The end of a very long fight that they both got to win.

There was the way he drew her with him up the stairs to the studio above the depot the way he had so many times before. The way it felt so different now. The way the dance changed when they were in private. The way they helped each other out of their clothes, slowly this time. Carefully.

As if all of this was sacred.

Not that it hadn't been from the start, but this time, they'd waited.

This time, they'd already been naked in a far more important sense than the clothes they wore when they'd walked in the door.

This time, the fact that he was head over heels in love with her wasn't something he was going to have to fight to keep to himself.

And the fact that she was here, that she'd said what she'd said to him tonight, let him know that Sydney knew the truth of what he'd said to her.

Fully.

He picked her up and carried her over to his bed. Then he laid her out on top of it, coming down with her so he could move beside her, then take his sweet time learning every last inch of her.

As if this was new.

They were laughing, because it *felt* so new. So different.

So perfect.

"You amaze me," she managed to say as he trailed heat and longing and love all over her body.

"Not as much as you amaze me," he said, grinning up at her as he settled between her legs.

And the first time he made her buck and moan, then shatter into a million pieces, it felt like light.

When she came back to herself he was pulling her beneath him, but she stopped him, framing his face with her hands, and looking at him with her eyes wide and serious and still half dazed.

The most beautiful face he'd ever seen.

"I think I always have," she told him.

And he knew what she meant. But he let the corner of his mouth crook up anyway, and shook his head just slightly.

"Darlin'," he said, "it's been a long time coming. I'm going to need those words."

She laughed a little, and flushed at the same time. "I deserve that. If you want to make it hard for me, I understand."

"Sydney. You don't need to worry about hard."

He was delighted by the way she laughed at that, as if she was a silly little thing without a thought in the world but him, this bed, and what they could do here. It was a new kind of magic to hear laughter like that out of her mouth and to see it echoed in those clever eyes of hers.

He had to think about farming implements. Intensely.

Because he really did need those words.

"Jackson," she said, with only a trace of laughter still in her voice, though her eyes grew solemn. "I love you. And I don't know how I'm going to stop being scared of that, or what on earth we're going to do, but I'm here. For at least four months. And I promise you, I'm going to be in it, with you, the whole time."

"We'll be in it together," he promised her.

Then he slid himself home, deep and true.

With slow, unhurried strokes, he took her apart all over again, built her back up—and then let them both fly free.

And when they woke up again they were tangled up in each other, and she was starving, as usual.

So he went and pulled together some food. A little bit of pasta, some astonishingly good bread from the bakery nearby, beer from his brewery. And she didn't lie in the bed and ask him arch little questions that were designed to prevent intimacy, not encourage it. Not tonight.

Tonight she came into the kitchen space of the studio, wearing his T-shirt like it was hers, and hiked herself up on the counter so she could sit with him while he put together a meal.

Like she wanted that as much as he did, that closeness.

He spent the rest of the night showing her just how close they could be.

When he woke in the morning, the light was pouring in. It was another beautiful day, and he could see the big, blue Montana sky that never failed to make his heart lift.

But that was nothing next to the sight of the woman still sleeping next to him, right there in his bed. She hadn't snuck back to her hotel. She hadn't kissed him on her way out, her gaze already cool.

She was *right here.*

He studied Sydney Campbell there beside him, dressed in nothing but sunshine, and he knew that it was all going to be okay.

More than okay.

They were going to figure it out. He was going to live a life filled with moments like this. She'd given him four months, but he had every intention of making it a lifetime.

And maybe that was all over his face when she stirred sometime later, because the way she smiled at him felt like a vow.

She blinked, as if she couldn't quite understand why it was so bright.

Then her smile widened, because she knew.

Because she could see all the things he could see. Jackson was sure of it.

So he leaned over and he kissed the love of his life *hello* on the first morning of the rest of their lives.

"It's daylight, baby," he told her, his mouth against hers and no distance between them, not even the slightest inch. Not ever again. "Welcome home."

# Chapter Eleven

SYDNEY DIDN'T KNOW what most people did after they told someone they loved them, then had it declared right back.

But what she and Jackson did was go to the rodeo.

She sat with him in the stands, pressed up close to watch event after event while Jackson sat next to her and told her what was happening. Why it was important. Why it was emotional and fun and why people turned out for this year after year. Why some people followed rodeos all around. He was better than any sportscaster could ever be.

They went to the steak dinner that night, put on as a fundraiser for the Cattleman's Association. He held her hand as he greeted the usual crowd of people who came up to speak to him, and that was that, then.

He wasn't hiding her. She didn't want him to.

But she'd certainly never… had a *boyfriend* before.

The word didn't seem to fit a man like Jackson. That was probably why Luce insisted on using it. To Sydney's face all Saturday, and apparently in a barrage of texts to the entire family, too.

"You have a boyfriend?" Devyn demanded when she

called that Sunday morning.

"I do," Sydney said, grinning at Jackson, who was standing right next to her in the studio, and could hear every word.

And just like when she'd asked him on that date, she had a moment of freezing panic that he would shake his head and disabuse her of the notion that they were anything like *boyfriend and girlfriend*—but instead, he grinned.

Like the notion delighted him.

"But more importantly, I'm off to stuff my face with pancakes," she told her sister. "Apparently, it's a rodeo tradition."

"You have a boyfriend and you're going to a rodeo with *pancakes*," Devyn breathed.

"We need to get moving," Jackson rumbled, in a way Devyn was sure to hear. "Because they get a crowd and I do love me some bacon."

As they walked out of the depot building, she tried to really hold the reality that the rest of her family already knew that Sydney, the most unlikely of them all to find anyone, had gone ahead and done it anyway. Thanks to Marietta, like most of the rest of them.

She would have sworn it would never happen. That she really was cursed and would die first.

But that was the funny thing about flinging herself into the unknown like this. She was already in so much trouble where Jackson was concerned, because if this didn't work out, it would devastate her. She understood that.

Yet she also understood that she'd been a fool to think that breaking up sooner rather than later would help. It wouldn't.

Jackson Flint was either going to cast a light or a shadow over the rest of her life. That was a fact. And there was no use fretting about which it was going to be now.

So she settled in. And she enjoyed her pancakes.

The same way she intended to enjoy the rest of her four months here.

She met Carol Bingley, who reminded her of Elly except perhaps less grim, and applauded her and her Woman of the Year award. She met Ansley Campbell, no relation, who she liked immediately because she had the good sense to think highly of Jackson.

Since she agreed, and Ansley seemed to have eyes for another rancher, she thought they'd get along fine.

She got a full-on interrogation, not from Jasper Flint and Mayor Chelsea, but from Jackson's two nephews and one niece, all of whom made it clear that they were the committee that mattered when it came to the Flint family's affections.

"I'll do my best to impress you," she told them, solemnly.

The little girl looked doubtful. The middle boy laughed. And the eldest one stared back at her, solemnly.

"We're going to have to take a vote," he told her. "And I

don't like your chances."

When the rodeo left town, everything seemed to settle down. Not just in terms of fewer people in town, but because the Copper Mountain Rodeo was clearly a turning point in the Marietta year. Once it was done, it seemed that even the weather stopped cooperating. It started to get much colder at night. And then in the mornings, too.

And soon enough, there was snow in the hills and warnings of hard frosts and snow in the valley, too.

"If you're only going to be here for a few months," Jackson said one day, very lazily, when she was repacking her clothes for the millionth time, "why don't you just stay with me?"

Sydney had another moment of that same old panic. Because she wanted nothing more than to move in with him, even if it was only temporary.

But… what would everyone think? Would they roll their eyes and say they knew it all along—that in the end, she was just like her mother?

Then she remembered.

She didn't have to hold on to tight to the past. She didn't have to hold on at all. That wasn't her job. And if she really wanted to be like her mother, she should remember that Melody had always, always tried to follow her heart, no matter where it led.

It was the *no matter who it hurt* part that had always gotten her upset, as Melody's daughter. But there was something beautiful about opening a heart like that, again and again, heedless of what came before.

That was something she could stand to learn from her mother.

Maybe someday she'd even tell her so.

Sydney moved into the studio at the depot, and found that as much as she'd liked her beautiful room at the Graff, she was happy to leave it behind.

Because in Jackson's home, she spent no time at all staring at the ceiling in the middle of the night, wishing she was with him. In Jackson's home, all she had to do was roll over and he was there.

She felt like she was getting away with something.

Sydney spent her days at her family breakfasts. And also helping Luce and Luce's friends with their various computer issues. She did so much of this that it soon became clear that if she really wanted to, she could set up some kind of cottage industry here in Marietta. Because it turned out that all of the time she'd spent analyzing complicated things and breaking them down for her superiors made her very good at explaining technology to people who found it scary and overwhelming. And in the evenings, she usually had a shift at Grey's.

Her uncle Jason never spoke of her relationship with Jackson again. She almost wished that he would. She could tell him that he was wrong. She didn't know *how* he was wrong, because she wasn't looking past the four months she and Jackson had promised each other, but he was wrong all the same.

But she had other things to concentrate on when it came to her uncle, namely her grandparents. Jason surprised everyone in November by inviting any family in the area to come over for Thanksgiving. Even Uncle Billy and his family came in from Billings. And after they'd all eaten and argued over whose sweet potatoes were better, then taken the usual phone calls and video calls from far and near, he led them all out into the frigid backyard and showed them that he'd built a tiny little house back there, down by the river.

"Are you opening up the hotel business?" Elly asked, somewhere between arch and amused.

But she was different too, their frosty grandma. Things had changed this fall. Elly Grey was never going to turn cozy, but she was softer, all the same.

"I'm going to live in it myself," Jason said. Then he penned his mother with that hard look of his that made drunks stop in their tracks. "And you and Dad are going to move back into the house and stay here in town. Big Sky is too far."

Sydney and Luce stared at each other. Jackson, who was taking her off to Flathead Lake to meet his brother Jonah and his wife and kids later this Thanksgiving weekend, put a hand on her back in silent support.

They all expected Grandma to bite Jason's head off. At the very least.

Instead, Elly inclined her head. And then shocked everyone further by reaching over and taking Richard's hand.

"It would be nice," she said, haltingly, "to come home."

And the uncles had them moved in before Christmas.

It was a different Christmas, because it wasn't in Big Sky, the way it had been for so long. All of her cousins, all of her aunts and uncles, made this new Marietta Grey family Christmas the kind of party that swept from one house to the next.

One cold, snowy afternoon after Christmas she found herself with Devyn, walking back toward Uncle Jason's house—now Grandma and Grandpa's house—from a snowshoeing expedition down by the river, both of them red cheeked and bright eyed.

"You seem happy," Devyn said. She pressed her shoulder to Sydney's. "I'll be honest. I didn't think that was something you could be."

Sydney smiled. "Neither did I."

And they probably would have cried, the pair of them, but it was too cold for that. The tears would only freeze on their eyelids, so they settled for grinning at each other a little tearfully instead. Then racing each other home.

On New Year's Eve, when Sydney had checked in with work and was dreading the day she might have to actually think about leaving, she and Jackson went to the party his brother and Chelsea were throwing up at the old Crawford mansion. They dressed in pretty clothes. They danced and toasted the new year.

It was glittery and happy. It was perfect.

And when they got back to the train depot that already felt like hers, this man of hers got down on one knee, looked up at her, and grinned.

"I love you," he said, the way he always did. Again and again, so there could be no mistake. And so she would say it back. Or say it first. Which she did. "I want you to marry me. If you need me to move back to DC, I will. But darlin', I think you should stay."

Sydney didn't analyze it. She didn't triangulate data points or consult sources.

She simply followed her heart.

"I love you too," she told him, already smiling so hard it should have hurt. "I think you should definitely marry me. And I think I'm ready to be one of the Greys of Marietta who lives right here."

"Baby. Just one word. But you need to say it."

Sydney laughed, and this time, she knew that what she felt inside her wasn't a bruise. It was tenderness. It was love. It hurt exactly the way it was supposed to, and that was the point.

"Then you need to ask," she told him.

He liked that. He repositioned the small box he was holding, with a stone that looked as bright as Sydney felt. "Sydney Campbell, you beautiful woman, I want to love you forever," he said. "Will you marry me?"

"Jackson Flint, you are the love of my life," she told him right back, leaning close so she could get her hands on him. On his gorgeous face. "Yes, I will marry you. I can't wait."

"I guess that settles it," Jackson drawled, but that grin of his was breaking his face wide open.

Then he swept her up in his arms, and she wrapped herself around him like she never planned to let go, and they spent the rest of their lives working on the best part.

The happy ever after part.

Better still, they got it right.

And it didn't take seventy years.

## The End

## The 85th Copper Mountain Rodeo Series

Book 1: *Take Me Please, Cowboy* by Jane Porter

Book 2: *Tempt Me Please, Cowboy* by Megan Crane

Book 3: *Marry Me Please, Cowboy* by Sinclair Jayne

Book 4: *Promise Me Please, Cowboy* by C.J. Carmichael

See Carol Bingley's story in....
*The Untold Story of Carol Bingley* by Jane Hartley

# Exclusive Excerpt: Marry Me Please, Cowboy

The next book in the 85th Copper Mountain Rodeo series

THE SLIDE OF metal just before the chute opened was the best sound in the world. But, no lie, it was potentially the most ominous. Today the hard hit and clang of metal—like a dozen miners hitting a vein of iron ore—heralded potential disaster. Two thousand pounds of bull crashed into the chute gate as Blasphemous's horn hooked metal. The huge head dipped before rearing back in panic, forcing Huck Jones to angle nearly parallel along the thrashing bull's spine. The gasps, shouts and shrieks messed with his whole keep-calm-and-carry-on rodeo cowboy vibe because his next move could get him killed.

That would be an unpleasant irony—he'd spent nearly a decade slipping in and out of global hotspots as army Special Forces only to bite it on the back of a bull in front of a bunch of summer tourists.

Huck Jones hit the dirt, rolled and clamored to the top of the chute gate as the same angry and disoriented two thousand pounds spun around to charge back into the chute. Huck hopped to the other side of the chute and dropped down to safety, not even breathing hard.

Not the best debut on the Montana circuit at the Northwest Montana Fair & Rodeo in Kalispell, but since he was still vertical and breathing with nothing broken, not the worst.

He thought of the colorful blue words his brothers in arms would have shouted seeing that disastrous rollout but swallowed them. He shook with the flood of adrenaline and slapped his hat against his thigh—no helmet for him—he'd had to wear one for too many years in Special Forces. It felt too good to wear the black Resistol Cody Johnson that his foster granddad had kept safe for him through his multiple deployments. He did wear a mouth guard because Jim Austin, the old-school rancher outside of Cody, Wyoming, who'd taken him in at thirteen, had forked out eight grand for his first ever dental work and braces.

He'd also taught him how to read, do the ranch's books and study before giving him his first taste of public school when he enrolled him in his freshman year of high school after a year of intensive work to 'get him up to speed.' Jim had also taught him how to be a steward of the land and animals, finish what he started and to treat himself and others with respect, and how to pray, which is probably what he should be doing right about now.

"That sure was something to see." Jim, stood—still looking fit at seventy-five—on top of the chute and stared down at him, subtly checking for injuries.

Huck tongued out his mouth guard so he could speak. "Happy to amuse you."

"I ain't amused. Buckin' broncs don't got horns and after what you've been through, I'd hoped you'd lost your taste for danger."

Huck didn't have a taste for danger. He'd just wanted to pit his skills against a bull's. He'd been practicing this summer and had accrued enough points to try it at this rodeo, and he hated that he wouldn't get a score.

"You still intent on showing off?"

"Pretty sure that was an epic fail." He tried to keep the disappointment out of his voice. Sure, he'd ridden bulls and broncs as a teen, but this summer, his first out of the service, he and Jim had spent most weekends on the Wyoming rodeo circuit—kind of a bucket list for both of them. He'd had quite a bit of success steer wrestling and saddle-bronc riding, but bull riding had been tapping his shoulder. The purse was bigger and the points on the bull combined with the other events would guarantee his entry into the Copper Mountain Rodeo in Marietta, Montana, next weekend.

"Not necessarily," Jim drawled. "Bull's disqualified," he said laconically. "You going to give it another go?"

His thigh hurt where a hoof had caught him. His hip and ribs hurt from hitting the dirt, and he'd twisted his right wrist in the grip when he'd kicked out. Maybe he should stick to saddle broncs, but he'd been practicing on bulls during the Cody Nite Rodeo series all August and was getting a taste for it that he probably shouldn't.

"Heck yes, sir."

Jim gave a slight nod to the judging panel, and Huck heard his name announced and the crowd's cheers as another bull was led through the chute—not the one he'd ride, another cowboy was already queued up. But he'd get another shot today, and that was all a cowboy, and his mentor, who was also checking off another dream, could ask for.

He gave a final look at Jim, toothpick in his mouth—no longer the disgusting chew, finally, after his first dance with cancer three years ago. Turning away, Huck jammed his hat back on his head and walked toward his duffel to rewrap his thumb that felt like it had pulled out of the socket again. The ribbing from the other cowboys, who were regulars on the Montana circuit, which he certainly was not, was all part of the experience. He allowed the teasing to roll off him and mouthed off a few one-liners of his own.

Spending the summer honing his skills at the local weekend rodeos in Dubois or Cody when not competing on the Wyoming rodeo circuit had been something he and Jim could do together while they each faced a major life decision. Huck—what he was going to do after nearly ten years in the army and Jim—was he going to hand over full control of his cattle ranch to his great-nephews, both of whom had finished college and graduate school—one in ranch management and the other in agriculture. They'd come to work for Jim a couple of years ago.

Summer was easing into fall. Huck had been sent home on a forced medical leave by a team of doctors and army psychiatrists after a mission had gone deeply south resulting in his team leader's death. Huck had been offered the chance to muster out early with ten years being served, but he was no closer to a decision about his future.

He'd hoped to work alongside Jim on his ranch, but Huck suspected Jim had had another health scare he wouldn't discuss and was easing out of running his ranch with an iron fist. The great-nephews were smart, good men. Wyoming born and bred and blood family. They had a right to the legacy. He wasn't and didn't. After a week 'home,' seeing Jim visibly aged and suspecting the cancer might be back, Huck had let go of the Wyoming ranch dream. Still he'd signed his papers to muster out, determined to help Jim with whatever he needed or wanted.

Jim had been there for him.

But they were in Montana for this weekend through next because Huck had a promise to keep to his brothers from his unit—the Coyote Cowboys—and the brother they'd lost, Jace McBride. Jace had left a list of amends and Huck was determined to do whatever it took to settle that score for Jace.

Find out what happens next…

Get now!

# More by Megan Crane

## The Flint Brothers Take Montana series

*Tempt Me, Cowboy*

*Please Me, Cowboy*

## The Greys of Montana Series

Book 1: *Come Home for Christmas, Cowboy*
Christina Grey's story

Book 2: *In Bed with the Bachelor*
Jesse Grey's story

Book 3: *Project Virgin*
Scottie Grey's story

Book 4: *Cody*
Skylar Grey's story

Book 5: *Have Yourself a Crazy Little Christmas*
Devyn Voss's story

## Standalone titles

*Game of Brides*

*I Love the 80s*

*Once More with Feeling*

## About the Author

USA Today bestselling, RITA-nominated, and critically-acclaimed author Megan Crane has written more than seventy-five books since her debut in 2004. She has been published by a variety of publishers, including each of New York's Big Five. She's won fans with her women's fiction, chick lit, and work-for-hire young adult novels as well as with the Harlequin Presents she writes as Caitlin Crews. These days her focus is on contemporary romance from small town to international glamor, cowboys to bikers, and beyond. She sometimes teaches creative writing classes both online at mediabistro.com and at UCLA Extension's prestigious Writers' Program, where she finally utilizes the MA and PhD in English Literature she received from the University of York in York, England. She currently lives in the Pacific Northwest with a husband who draws comics and animation storyboards and their menagerie of ridiculous animals. For more info visit her at www.megancrane.com or www.caitlincrews.com.

Thank you for reading

# Tempt Me Please, Cowboy

If you enjoyed this book, you can find more from all our great authors at TulePublishing.com, or from your favorite online retailer.

TULE

PUBLISHING

Made in the USA
Coppell, TX
03 October 2023

22355270R00118